Reprise

by

Claire Davon

Reprise

Cover Art by *Kim Mendoza*

The Wild Rose Press, Inc.
PO Box 708
Adams Basin, NY 14410-0708
Visit us at www.thewildrosepress.com

Publishing History
First Champagne Rose Edition, 2020
Trade Paperback ISBN 978-1-5092-3325-0
Digital ISBN 978-1-5092-3326-7

Published in the United States of America

She met Clarke's green gaze, and he returned the stare without blinking. Kai's attention fixed on the two of them, but he said nothing.

After a moment, she dropped her gaze and nodded. "We don't have a budget." Her tone was sharp. "This is all we can afford. Besides, it doesn't matter," she continued, tossing her head. Normally this gesture would make her hair wave, drawing male attention. Since Clarke started, she had kept her hair clipped back, and the movement didn't have its usual impact. "It's all about the downloads these days—streaming is where it's at. I am not even sure why we put out CDs. Cover art is irrelevant."

"That's untrue." Clarke shook his head with unexpected vehemence. "There's a whole underground movement toward great art, even if most is only a thumbnail. It's more important than ever. We only have a few seconds to grab someone's attention when they're scrolling through their online stores. Good cover art can make a person pause and take a chance. We've got to grab their attention, or the consumer moves on to the next cat video. This doesn't seize anything. We have to get them by the balls and make it imperative for them to download at least one song. Then we have them," he countered, folding his arms across his chest. The gesture accentuated his strong pectorals and biceps, and a shiver went down Terri's spine. "People love artwork. You can never predict what will catch on. Lots of things go viral."

He's an addict, she told herself. *He's a washed-up former celebrity who can't get anyone to answer his calls.*

He called you his little Maine stalker.

Dedication

To everyone who read this story through the years
as it changed and grew.
It has been quite a journey!

Chapter One

Terri never expected to come face-to-face with her past at a work party.

One moment she was making idle conversation with the VP of marketing at Shatter Sound, a rival record label. The next she was staring at the man she'd hoped never to see again.

All conversation stilled around her. Or perhaps that was just her former self shrieking. She felt as if she were a split screen in a movie—part of her extending her hand to shake and the other doing an impression of Munch's *The Scream*.

She waited for the explosion. Clarke Masters had made it abundantly clear ten years ago that he wanted nothing to do with the woman who always turned up where he was, trying to get his attention with increasingly desperate moves. What had he called her? Right. How could she forget.

My little Maine stalker.

Maybe he wouldn't make a scene. Maybe he'd give her a sneer and a dismissive sniff before turning away. Maybe he wouldn't reveal to the world what a boundary-smashing nightmare she'd been in her early twenties, before she'd gotten healthier and stronger.

It happened in slow motion. Her hand went toward Clarke's as she held her breath, waiting for the shock of recognition in his eyes. She hadn't changed that much.

Her hair was back to its natural red-gold color instead of platinum blond, and she'd put on a few pounds from her rock-and-roll groupie weight, but her face was the same as it had been ten years prior. A few more lines, sure, but that happened to everyone.

"Terri August," she said when their palms met. Her heart was pounding so hard she was sure those around her could make it out. Fear curled low in her stomach. The fight-or-flight reaction had her wanting to head for the open door of the patio they were standing on, but she remained where she was.

Better to get it over with. The upside was now she didn't have to fear running into him. It had happened.

"Clarke Masters," he said with a cool handshake and a neutral smile. "Nice to meet you, Terri August. What brings you here? Work?"

She waited a heartbeat too long. What would he say next? Maybe he would call her Lynx—the pseudonym she had gone by back then—and say…what? It was hard to imagine. She'd had a million scenarios play out in her mind, but never this one. Rock stars, even fallen ones, didn't go to office parties.

A second stretched into two, pushed into what was about to be an uncomfortable silence. She stared, unable to stop herself, as the only thing that made sense manifested. The VP of marketing, a man whose name she didn't remember, introduced himself to Clarke as a roaring in her ears engulfed everything else. Only one possible reason for his response came to mind.

Clarke didn't recognize her.

"Yes," she managed, with no clear idea of how she got words out. "I'm with Apposite Records." She pointed to her boss, who was in a corner chatting with a woman Terri hadn't met. Kai raised his glass to her before turning back to his companion.

Clarke followed her gaze to Kai before focusing on her. The fight-or-flight instinct intensified until it was all she could do to stay in one spot.

She had hoped he would look ragged, but time had not diminished him. He was still tall, his body showing the effects of working out in strong shoulders and powerful thighs. His hair was shorter and thinner than his rock-star days and now was cut just above his neck. Lines radiated out from his eyes. Similar marks bracketed those lush, full lips her teenage self had dreamed of. Wild living had taken its toll after all. He was no longer the young, limber man he had once been. The change wasn't enough. She had contemplated far worse in the dark revenge fantasies that haunted her mind in the middle of the night.

"Got it." He raised an eyebrow.

His cool, almost professional gaze took in her body with a detached air, sweeping from her calves to her hair in a manner that left Terri wanting to fidget with the long locks. She had tied it back as she usually did, leaving her nothing to do with her hands.

"Well, then I guess it's good we met now." Clarke's appraisal ended, and he gave her a brisk nod.

Kai detached from the woman, bowing to her before starting on an intercept course toward them. The cocktail party had begun two hours ago and was winding down. Clarke had a glass that fizzed like sparkling water and not alcohol. Rumor had it he had gone to rehab and gotten clean. She tried to remember the timing but couldn't. At one time in her life, she could have told a person anything they wanted to know about the lead singer of Attraction.

Before she could ask what Clarke meant, Kai was there, clapping the other man on the back in a gesture that spoke of familiarity and friendship. She stared at first one man and then the other.

"Clarke, this is Terri August, my vice president and indispensable second-in-command. Terri, this is Clarke Masters."

Of the people in her life today, only her family and Ally knew her history with the former rock star. Most of the time she tried not to remember the person she had been.

"We met," she said, her mouth dry. She searched for the drink she had set down, but it had been taken by a zealous waiter. The bar was a million miles away.

"Just now," Clarke agreed, a line forming between his eyebrows.

Although she was fighting to keep a calm exterior, she must be radiating tension. With every passing moment she expected him to say, "Ah-ha," and sniff with disgust.

"Good, good." Kai cuffed Clarke lightly on the arm. "I was hoping you would make it. I wanted to introduce you guys before tomorrow."

She blinked. Tomorrow? What was tomorrow? She waited for Clarke's explosive burst of recognition, the accusing glare when he realized who he was dealing with. *Little Maine stalker.*

Instead he studied her with a puzzled question in his eyes, as if she was familiar, but he couldn't place why. His teeth flashed at Kai's statement. They were white and straight, the product of teenage braces, if her avid research at that time was correct. "Dude, she's looking at you like you are from another planet. Didn't you tell her?"

His voice, roughened from years of abuse, still had a silken tone. The notes moved over her like the ripple of a wave, sending unexpected chills up her spine.

Surprise and disappointment warred within her, in equal parts dismay and relief. She had prepared and discarded a thousand clever sentences should she ever be in his presence again. The careful plotting had been for nothing. He had no idea who she was.

She swallowed, trying to focus on the conversation. "Um. Tell me what?"

A passing waiter offered them glasses of wine, and Terri snatched a white off the tray, wanting to down it in one gulp. Neither Kai nor Clarke accepted a drink.

The roaring in her ears intensified, and it took her a moment to realize it was the surf. The patio of the Santa Monica hotel made it a perfect place to observe the waves, but she'd forgotten they were there.

Kai smiled, the appearance of a person who clearly expected to be rewarded for his next words. "You can't keep going the way you have been, Terri." He slung an arm around her and hugged her briefly.

She stood frozen, a slow realization beginning to take root in her mind. No. It wasn't possible. Surely Kai wouldn't make personnel decisions without her. She normally did the bulk of the HR stuff in their office. She would have known.

"I...I get by," she said, just above a whisper.

She was afraid the stem of the glass would break the way she was holding it. She took another sip and disposed of it on a nearby table, focusing on the two men.

"You're drowning. I got you some help. Clarke is the new A&R guy. He's going to shake things up, find us some new bands. He starts tomorrow."

"To…" She trailed off, apparently only able to speak in incomplete sentences.

Kai grinned, smoothing his hand over his scalp. "If you need anything, Terri is your gal." His black hair bobbed when he half bowed. "We would have failed a long time ago without her. We're—I'm—grateful she's with us."

She flicked her hand in thanks, her face growing hot. Clarke was still examining her when she met his gaze. The piercing green of his eyes jumped out at her, without the redness of alcohol and drugs. The shorter hair made them more prominent.

The whole incident ten years ago had filled her with so much shame that she never considered Clarke Masters wouldn't know her. The sordid past had taken up free rent in her head, and she assumed the same was true of him.

Apparently not.

A million retorts danced through her mind before she mentally smoothed down her skirt and flicked her attention back to the duo.

"Well, nothing like springing a surprise on your VP the day before someone starts." She had no idea how she wrenched the innocent-sounding sentences out of her brain. "I guess I should be grateful he didn't turn up in the office and leave me completely unprepared, instead of just taken off guard." She cleared her throat and inclined her head to Clarke.

To her surprise relief flashed across his face.

"Welcome to Apposite Records. We're small but

mighty. That's what Kai says."

Clarke flashed her a smile that she remembered from long ago. Terri shut down the part of her brain that would have once done anything for a look like that from him. He was only Clarke Masters. Not a god. Just a man. He didn't remember her. The ugly incident might never have happened. The knowledge should have been a relief.

"Thanks," he said and shared a glance with Kai. "Happy to help."

She hoped she was making sense as they continued to talk. One neon blinking sign kept flashing across her mental vision with the inescapable truth.

Clarke Masters was coming to work for Apposite Records. And there was nothing she could do about it.

The next morning, after watching the clock tick toward nine, Terri finally hurled her notepad across the room in frustration. The book made a dull thud against the wall, scoring the plaster with its edge before flopping down to the floor. The notebook had been a gift from Kai. The front cover read *Life begins at the end of your comfort zone*. She was aware he'd given the pad to her as a subtle reminder to stretch her boundaries. She was quite happy in her comfort zone. Maybe she should replace the thing with one of those wide-lined notebooks, the ones that reminded her of high school. Sighing, she went to her desk and plopped into her leather executive chair.

Clarke Masters.

Damn it.

She moved documents from one pile to another, reminding her of the damning legal one she'd received years ago. The letter the legal firm had sent her ten years ago was still filed in her home office somewhere. She hadn't thrown the official document away. The envelope with the green certified strip was a reminder of what an idiot she'd been. If she doubted what happened when she let her guard down, all she had to do was get the file to remind her. She had waited for months for a restraining order notification from the court, but nothing else had ever happened. While the order had long ago expired, there was no statute of limitations on being a moron.

She couldn't explain why her younger self had been so obsessed with Clarke Masters. The man was a jerk. His band had dumped him when he hit bottom. He was not the larger-than-life rock star who had been plastered across billboards and CD covers. The events were ten years ago, for heaven's sake. Ancient history.

She twisted her hair into a knot at the nape of her neck and secured the mass with a clip. *Accept what you cannot change, Terri. Forget the past and get to work.*

Still, she found irony in the fact that the man who fronted a band that had had five number-one hits in a row was now forced to take an A&R—sic—social media job with a struggling record label. She doubted he was popular with the strippers now. He had few friends, but one of them was her boss. She had no idea who Kai spent time with. In the five years she had been in his life, Kai always kept his business and private lives separate. Apparently Clarke Masters was one of his inner circle.

Terri got up from her desk to retrieve her notebook. Clarke was a member of the team. She couldn't change that, so she had to accept it. She let out a sigh and turned her attention to the pile of work on her desk.

****

Clarke took in the room containing a desk and credenza, a computer in a docking station, and a phone with a headset. Two burgundy and brown guest chairs sat in front, appearing a bit worn. He wasn't the first person to have those chairs grace his office. He slung his leather satchel off his shoulder and onto the floor.

Nobody was there to witness the dismay he now let show on his face. He worked for *the man*. Clarke Masters had joined the nine-to-five.

From an early age he had planned his life so he wouldn't have to be on a schedule. He used to say being tied to a desk was a slow death. Even in high school, with the arrogance of the young, he had told people if he didn't become a famous rock star, he would rather dig ditches than work at an office.

Young Clarke was such a tool. Conceited and full of himself, he thought he ruled the world. When he crashed, he'd taken everything down with him. He was lucky he had any options at all. Kai's unexpected offer had been what AA called a "God shot." He hadn't taken the job for the money but for redemption in the eyes of those who judged him.

People like Terri August. The way she'd glared at him made Clarke shudder. She'd tried to hide her emotions, but she hadn't done a very good job. He didn't think they'd ever met, but she acted like he'd killed her dog. Maybe they'd had sex long ago. Plenty of women were in that category.

Maybe she'd lost family members to the disease of alcoholism and didn't trust a former addict. At one time the disapproval of anyone who was not a stunning model or actress wouldn't have mattered. The models hadn't lasted, but he hadn't cared. There'd always been another one. Then there hadn't been. When the band dumped him and his star faded, they'd stopped answering the phone or returning his calls. They'd ignored him at clubs, dismissing him from their circle as he once dismissed people like Terri. Hollywood was a brutal place for people who crashed and burned.

Terri wasn't a ten by any means. She was average, at best pretty, but no supermodel. Her gray eyes, which had taken him in and judged him, were large and nicely shaped. A lot of reddish-blond hair had been swept up behind a big, last-decade clip. Her bland jacket and slacks fit fine. She was of average height and weight, no lush curves or enhanced breasts to draw his attention.

In the past he would have flashed her his practiced Clarke Masters flirty grin, given her the once-over, and dismissed her from his mind. Idly, he tried to imagine Terri naked. What would she be like open and begging for him? Would she be a hellion, or was she a lousy lay? To his surprise, his penis reacted, twitching to life. Sweat dotted his forehead, and he hardened to a semi-erect state.

Fat chance of that, Masters.

He sat in the ergonomic desk chair, feeling the mesh of the back support against his shirt. The docked laptop made a reassuring whir when he thumbed the power button on and waited for the computer to load the main menu.

Visible through the door was a cubicle that held a gray-haired, older woman. The officious Terri had informed him her name was Sunshine. He'd had assistants before, ones that helped him get drugs and alcohol. They tidied up after him, shooed unwanted guests out, and went on snack runs. They handled paperwork, doing the stuff he was too far gone to handle. But a secretary? He didn't have the faintest clue what to do with her.

"Do you have a minute?" Kai asked, neither in nor out of the office.

Clarke gestured to the bare desk. "I think I can clear my schedule," he said with a wry twist to his lips.

"Good, good." Kai closed the door and sat in one of the guest chairs, his posture straight. "I owe you my thanks."

Clarke waved a hand in a self-deprecating gesture. "Not needed. You think this"—his arms took in the company beyond his office—"will work?"

Kai smoothed a hand through his black hair. The strands shifted and then fell back into place with the movement. "I don't know." He followed Clarke's wave, his face impassive. "We can only try. The gossip sites have taken notice." He turned his phone toward Clarke. "I made sure the avid gossip bloggers 'found out' about our new partnership. I've pulled a few strings to get the attention of the smaller columns. Once one of them picks this up, the rest will follow."

Clarke fought to keep his face from showing anything but neutrality. "Despite what P.T. Barnum said, not all publicity is good publicity."

"I consider any publicity better than irrelevance. This label is one step above self-releasing. You're my last shot."

Clarke clenched his teeth, his jaw muscles flexing with the movement. Once he would have run from the responsibility of helping anyone. An image of red-gold hair lodged in his brain. Terri August was no doubt good at it, unlike him. "Is your vice president in on this plan?"

"She's a great worker and a valued employee, but she does too much, and she's lost in the minutia. Terri is a bit rigid in her thinking. She's got a strong sense of right and wrong, but she's a professional, and we're in trouble. She'll work with you."

"She doesn't like me."

"She'll do what's needed." Kai's voice held the flat tone of command. He flashed Clarke a questioning look. "I'm surprised you guys didn't cross paths. From what little she's said, she haunted the rock clubs when she first got here. I think the Whammy Bar was one of them. She's pretty. The old Clarke would have charmed the pants off her."

Clarke winced, hoping the movement wasn't visible. His failure was evident when Kai's eyes softened and he turned his gaze from his face to a neutral point beyond Clarke.

"Hell, maybe she did know me, hence the distaste. Didn't you hear, man? The old Clarke went into a bottle and never came out."

Kai met his gaze again. Clarke was relieved that neither compassion nor condemnation showed in Kai's face. Clarke's past was his to own. His reputation as an asshole was well deserved.

"The new Clarke won't do that."

Unsure that Kai's trust was warranted, Clarke said nothing. His mind went to Terri again, but the enigma of Kai's second-in-command would have to wait for another day. "How are we going to save this company?"

"I'm hoping you can make the difference. If not, then there's nothing we can do."

The idea that anyone was giving him that much responsibility made the old Clarke want to turn and run, but he only nodded. "I'll do my best, man."

"That's all anyone can ask."

Chapter Two

Terri tried to ignore the murmur of voices next door. Clarke Masters didn't remember the child she had been, the overeager would-be girlfriend. The stalker. If he didn't know, she wasn't going to remind him.

Clarke had worked there less than a month, blowing into the office like a cool breeze, bringing stories and conversation. To her surprise he was a good listener, drawing each person out with interested murmurs and leading questions. That wasn't how it had been back when she interacted with him before. He'd held court, told stories, often at a rapid clip, and tended to get sloppy as the evening went on.

Most knew his past when he started, and those who didn't learned soon enough. She'd discovered that nobody cared after a few days. Terri would also have succumbed to Clarke's curiosity under different circumstances. She'd met his attempts to get to know her with bland, generic answers and a barrier she hoped he never tried to breach.

He had climbed a wall in his rock-star days, a publicity stunt for the last Attraction album. Terri had only read about the show; she hadn't dared go to the event. The letter had been fresh in her mind, and her psyche burned with hatred and shame.

Recipes. They always soothed her. Pushing Clarke out of her mind, she found the URL for one of the cooking channels. Maybe they had something interesting she hadn't tried yet.

She became aware that her messaging system light was blinking. Ally Wilson, one of Terri's few friends and the only person she still talked to who was privy to her past, was hailing her.

—How's it going?— Ally's IM said. *—Are you surviving Clarke showing up?—*

—It's still so weird he doesn't remember me. He has no idea who I am.—

—That's good, right?— Ally added a smiley face. *—It has to be a relief.—*

—Yeah.— Terri lied. *—It is.—*

—How are you holding up? Anything I can do?—

She considered revealing the truth about her bone-deep fear that she was going to get found out and ridiculed. Then she shook her head. No point in that.

—Nah, I'm good. I've been checking recipes. I want to do some pasta. I found this great recipe that uses radiatore. I'll need...hmm— Terri scanned the items needed in the dish she'd discovered on one of the sites. *—Feta and raisins. Tomatoes.—* Terri was also logging the items into her shopping app as she replied to Ally.

The cursor blinked for a few minutes before Ally replied. To her relief, her friend accepted the change in topic. *—Radiatore? Terri, you find the craziest things.—*

Terri grinned, even though her friend couldn't see her. *—The pasta is shaped like a radiator to hold the sauce. I had a heck of a time finding this noodle, so now I have to try. I'll let you know how my dish turns out.—*

She finished her list of needed ingredients. She

wouldn't share with anyone how gutted she felt. If she didn't give voice to her fears, they might not come true. Cooking would distract her. Anything was better than thinking about a man who had filled her dreams and then her nightmares, a man who didn't remember her at all. His lack of memory stung. Part of her perverse self wanted him to remember her, despite what that would mean.

She was a fool.

Her IM buzzed.

—*Got to go, Ally. It's Kai. He's got something to show me.*—

—*Catch you later.*—

When she arrived at Kai's office, he had artwork laid out across the desk. To her dismay, Clarke was there, peering at the images. She recognized her handiwork and tried not to flinch. Her rudimentary photo-editing skills were acceptable but by no means amazing.

Kai beckoned her forward, and she went, reluctance in every step she took. She tried to edge away from Clarke, but despite her efforts he was close enough for her to smell his cologne. She wished he'd gotten ugly, but all he'd done was age well, maturing from his youthful, aggressive good looks into someone who was conventionally handsome.

"What do you think?" Kai turned his attention to the other man, his posture intent.

Clarke eyed the potential album images. She had gone to stock picture websites online and taken clip art from the internet, stuff she could use for a nominal fee if they selected the image as the final version. Then she had superimposed the artist's face over the backgrounds, using her rudimentary editing skills to vary the colors and the size. The covers she'd come up with were basic, but they were also cheap.

Clarke stepped back from Terri and snorted. His warmth went with him, and the tingling dancing along her skin faded.

"What do I think? They're boring." He gestured to the images, and she knew what he meant. The clip art and the unsmiling image of the artist made them like every generic cover that littered the net.

She met Clarke's green gaze, and he returned the stare without blinking. Kai's attention fixed on the two of them, but he said nothing.

After a moment, she dropped her gaze and nodded. "We don't have a budget." Her tone was sharp. "This is all we can afford. Besides, it doesn't matter," she continued, tossing her head. Normally this gesture would make her hair wave, drawing male attention. Since Clarke started, she had kept her hair clipped back, and the movement didn't have its usual impact. "It's all about the downloads these days—streaming is where it's at. I am not even sure why we put out CDs. Cover art is irrelevant."

"That's untrue." Clarke shook his head with unexpected vehemence. "There's a whole underground movement toward great art, even if most is only a thumbnail. It's more important than ever. We only have a few seconds to grab someone's attention when they're scrolling through their online stores. Good cover art can make a person pause and take a chance. We've got to grab their attention, or the consumer moves on to the next cat video. This doesn't seize anything. We have to get them by the balls and make it imperative for them to download at least one song. Then we have them," he countered, folding his arms across his chest. The gesture accentuated his strong pectorals and biceps, and a shiver went down Terri's spine. "People love artwork. You can never predict what will catch on. Lots of things go viral."

He's an addict, she told herself. *He's a washed-up former celebrity who can't get anyone to answer his calls.*

He called you his little Maine stalker.

"Make the cover something they choose over the latest meme or sports score," Clarke continued. Motioning with his clasped arms, he waved to the conference table where the potential covers lay. "These won't stand out anywhere. They gain us nothing."

"I'm open to ideas, Clarke," Kai said, rolling over the top of Terri's "maybe you have something better?" Her voice was edged with scorn, and one eyebrow lifted in disbelief.

"I might. I have a friend," he began.

"You do?" The comment was out before she could stop herself.

Hurt flickered across his face. It cleared as she watched, replaced by a carefully neutral air.

"Nope, not in the end." He jerked a thumb at Kai. "Except this guy. He stuck with me. The rest I drove off." He gestured toward his office. "Be right back. I want to show you something."

After Clarke left, Kai studied Terri, his brow furrowed, his eyes narrowed.

She held up her hand. "I'm sorry. That was uncalled for."

"You need to learn to work together," he said in a

harsh tone. "You don't have to like him, but you have to deal with him. He's here to stay."

In the past years she'd gotten used to being called an essential employee of the company. She was someone Kai and Apposite relied on, but she was pushing her luck. Nobody was indispensable. Her composure and her livelihood had been threatened by a pair of green eyes and still impressive face and body. She assumed everyone would find Clarke to be a joke, but that crumbled when people spent time with him. In person he was charming and self-effacing, qualities he had never shown in his bombastic rock-star days. She'd forgotten what it was like to have that mesmerizing charm turned on her. In the ten years since she had been in his orbit, she had come to the conclusion that most of his appeal was due to his celebrity status, and now he had nothing to recommend him. The truth was Clarke still had the power to turn heads by walking into a room.

He reentered the room carrying sheets of photo paper. A faint tremor in his hands made the paper rustle. As he handed her pages, Terri wondered what he was doing. Lots of great images were out there, but they were all very expensive. Clarke had to be aware good artwork didn't come cheap.

She glanced down at the papers, her thoughts still occupied with the unwelcome awareness of Clarke. Then she blinked. Her mouth started to drop open, and she checked herself, closing her lips with a click of teeth.

She held abstract, stylized drawings in streaks of color. They leaped off the page in a dazzling torrent of visually stunning images. In one the glint of an eye and a slash of wolfish teeth lay buried in the forest. They evoked jungle and space and elemental simplicity wrapped around the outline of a face done in primary colors.

The artist friend, whoever he or she was, was amazingly talented. The person was so good that they had to be out of their price range. The idea was sound but futile.

Kai and Terri studied them in silence for several minutes. As one, they turned to Clarke.

His hands were resting on the conference table, but his fingertips were pressed into the wood so that his knuckles were bent. His shoulders were hunched forward. His full lips had thinned to slits, and his nostrils were flared.

He's nervous. Why?

"These are remarkable," she said in admiration.

Kai nodded in agreement, his black hair waving with the movement.

She continued. "Are they from that friend you mentioned?"

Clarke swallowed, a mix of emotions moving across his face. "Yeah. This guy isn't famous. He paints as a hobby, a way to relax. He's only shown his work to a handful of people."

Kai turned the closest picture around, pointing the image toward Clarke. "Would this person be willing to do something similar for our artist? We couldn't pay him much, but he might do it for the exposure."

Clarke's face lit up, but something guarded lurked in his appearance, a fragile air that belied the toothy grin.

Back in his heyday one of the things he had been

famous for was his smile. The beam was a broad grin of lips, teeth, and widened eyes, at once roguish and sexual.

She hadn't understood then how phony that gesture was. The grin was Clarke mugging for the camera, acting out his larger-than-life persona. This pleased, pensive one reached his eyes and settled in the lines radiating out from them and in the corners of his mouth. His new look was more mesmerizing than the old "hail fellow, well met" grin had ever been.

"I'll ask," Clarke said. "He's not the 'exposure is what people die of' type, but he'll want something. I'll get back to you in a few days. If our guy likes the idea, then we can talk about payment. I don't think his price will be outrageous."

****

The meeting broke up after that. There was nothing to say until they were informed if this mysterious artist would agree to a commission for a cover. Clarke could tell Terri was interested when her gaze kept flicking to the abstract picture. The approval in her eyes made an unexpected zing shoot down his nerve endings.

Fat chance of the guy saying no. Whether money was involved or not.

Clarke turned to his computer. He studied the pictures he had uploaded to the cloud for safe keeping. Pictures of all the paintings he had done in the last two years were there. The people in rehab had suggested he should have a hobby to fill his days—his hours— minutes, seconds. He had too much time and not enough structure otherwise. Since music wasn't a good idea, he'd chosen art. He painted savagely, throwing thick globs of oils and watercolors onto the canvas until the paint dripped down his arms as he worked out the desire for a drink or a drug one stroke at a time.

He swiveled around in his ergonomic chair until his mind whirled from the centrifugal force. He clasped his hands over the wood lip to make the rotation stop. Still, his head reeled, and he had to blink several times to clear his vision.

Terri liked his paintings.

He summoned up the picture she had focused on. The picture was his favorite too, an abstract of an artist in the program who was trying to get signed. Clarke wasn't sure how serious the guy was, but helping him had kept both of them sober. For a time.

Spinning around again, he stared out the window of the twelfth-story office. He'd gotten used to being there over the past month. If he dug below the surface, he liked the order being at the office brought to his day. The nine-to-five routine, rather than being stifling, gave him someplace to go. That was necessary for someone whose time could be measured in seconds spent trying not to use.

He shuffled through the papers on his desk until he found the tabloids advertising band gigs. Dog-eared pages and ads circled in black magic marker showed the bands he was interested in. He could have done the task online, but something about the cheap ink and the advertisements gave him satisfaction. Kai had given him carte blanche to check out acts and report any Clarke deemed worth pursuing. While he worked social media to get Apposite's name out there, he might as well do the job he was ostensibly hired to do. He might strike gold. He could find the Next Big Thing.

Tapping his pen on the paper, he sighed and ran his

free hand through his hair. He circled a band name without awareness of who he highlighted.

He doubted Terri would feel the same way about his paintings when she found out he was the artist. Many people hated him from his using days. All he could do was try and make things right—make amends as best he could. The reaction to his apologies had been mixed, with some refusing to listen to him and some dismissing his words as if they hadn't been needed. A few people, like his former guitarist Steve, forgave him but remained distant. Regrets could be accepted, but relationships were not so easily repaired.

Terri August's dislike cut him to the bone. With everyone else she was reserved but friendly, quick to take an interest in their personal lives but sharing little of her own. She was an enigma, her reserve making her difficult to pinpoint. She tried to avoid him, which wasn't possible in such a small space, but she made the effort to be absent if he was around.

Alcoholics Anonymous, the group he had been forced to go to as part of his rehab, taught him all he could do was ask for someone's forgiveness, and the rest was up to the other person. If he owed Terri August an apology, he had no idea what for.

He threw the marker down and started spinning the chair again. This was getting him nowhere. Terri was a self-righteous do-gooder who had no weaknesses. She had to have grown up in a perfect town with a cat and a dog and perfect siblings and parents. Her childhood house was as pristine as the rest, with a white picket fence and an impeccable lawn where no stray blade of grass would ever venture. Perfect friends and a perfect boyfriend...

Clarke was circling so fast squeaks emanated from the protesting chair. Grasping the edge of the desk, he brought himself to a halt.

She hadn't mentioned a man in the time he'd been there. She'd never been in a rush to leave the office, but there could be someone. Any man in Terri's life would be a Type A driven personality who had little time during the week for female companionship. He would be weekends only. That sort of arrangement would suit her.

Maybe on the weekends she loosened up. Maybe she took that pile of gorgeous-colored hair out of its clip and let the strands tumble down around her shoulders, framing her face with soft curls. He muttered an oath and turned back to his desk. Thinking about Terri would get him nowhere fast. She wasn't his type, and he sure as shit wasn't hers. Her reserve made her impossible to know—he had no idea what she did for fun. She was an enigma wrapped in a riddle. He was making too much out of her. She was not that complex. She was a workaholic with no social life, that was all.

The woman in question knocked on his open door, an uncertain expression on her face.

Clarke's body leaped to attention at the sight. The quickening shocked him with its ferocity. It had been a long time since he was with a woman and longer still that he'd been attracted to one. He'd had so little interest in the opposite sex in these past two years that he supposed his sexuality dead and buried. It sucked that the prickly Terri had caused his erection.

"Hey, you got a minute?" she asked, closing his office door behind her.

He nodded. Resting his body on the edge of his

desk, Clarke folded his arms and legs in front of him. "Sure, have a seat. What's on your mind, Terri?"

She sat in one of his burgundy and brown guest chairs, staring out the same window he had. Then she half smiled, but it died as he watched.

"I came to apologize." She flexed nervous fingers over padded armrests again and again.

He uncrossed his arms, his hands hanging loose at his sides. His mouth gaped open, and he just stared at her.

****

Clarke's shocked exhalation and subsequent silence erased the hope that she hadn't been as bad as she imagined. She twisted her hands over the chair arms again and didn't meet his gaze. "I haven't been fair to you. Your reputation precedes you, of course. But I've let that color my image of you." *Not to mention what happened ten years ago.* "Apposite is a long shot. Everyone knows it. The sharks circle in the press, waiting for our collapse. The only way we have any hope of making this work is by sticking together. You're..." She dared a glance Clarke's way and faltered at the gentle compassion there. She swallowed. "You're Kai's friend. Kai is the fairest, most decent man I've ever met. If he says you're okay, then that's good enough for me."

"Damn it. My reputation. Again. It follows me everywhere I go. I wish you had reason to think well of me other than just Kai's opinion." His face settled into harsh lines.

"I..." Surely she wasn't the only one to back away from him because of what had happened. Her opinion shouldn't carry that much weight. "Does it matter?"

25

He propelled himself off the desk and moved to crouch in front of her. "What if I said yes?"

His eyes were much too close, filling her vision with their green depths. She wanted to shout every time she laid eyes on him. Either that or kiss him.

"Why would my opinion mean anything?"

His gaze dropped to her mouth, and for a brief, wild moment, she thought he was going to kiss her. Her breath shortened at the idea of his lips on hers. Her former self would have rejoiced. This mature version was smarter than that.

Then he reared back and rose. Taking up his seat behind the desk again, he gave her a hooded glance. "I can't answer that. Apology accepted. I'm glad we can work together. I was getting tired of having to cut the air with a knife."

"Great. Thanks. Listen, are you hungry?" When his brows furrowed together at her non sequitur, she continued. "I…cook, and I tried this pulled pork recipe that was posted online." Damn, this was hard. "Following a recipe is easier if I make the whole thing and freeze the rest, but there's way too much. Would you like some? I think the dish is pretty good."

She waited, wishing she could retract the impulsively extended invitation. Trying to bury the hatchet was one thing, but spending time with him was insanity.

"You bake? I didn't see that coming. Why did you make the whole batch? With a mind like yours, I'm sure cutting the recipe in half would have been child's play."

"I cook," she corrected. "I don't often bake." Her inner critic mocked her. *Pedant.* She paused but then continued, afraid she would lose the nerve to speak. "Of course I could split the recipes, but cooking is relaxing for me. I don't want to spoil my mood by remembering what half of a tablespoon is, or halving all the protein, so I make them as written. I've got a big freezer."

The image of the classes at the Culinary Institute in Pasadena danced in her mind. It would be great to learn how to do the fancy stuff from the cooking shows, but she had never gotten further than checking out their website. The most she had ever done was try the videos online. Cooking was a hobby, that was all. Life didn't reward the frivolous. She remembered the time she'd brought cookies to a party at Attraction's bass player's house...Terri shuddered at the memory. Clarke's reaction had not been kind.

"If you eat with me, I'd love to try your dish. I'll warn you, though, one of my brothers is on the Ohio Pork Producers Council, so I know a thing or two about hogs."

"Really? Ohio?" Her long ago research indicated Clarke was from Southern California. "I'll heat it up." She fumbled for a safer topic. "Did you check out *Patsy Online* this morning? She talked about you on her blog and mentioned Apposite. We've gotten more publicity since you've been here than we did with our last release. I didn't think it would do any good, but your hire has definitely gotten us attention. I should be thanking you."

She was surprised when his gaze shifted away. The old Clarke would have loved the spotlight.

"That's what Kai is paying me for." His voice was muffled like he was suppressing deep emotion. "Come on, let's eat. I'm starved."

She wouldn't admit to him how much his approval meant, but warmth burrowed inside her at his easy acceptance of her offer. His opinion shouldn't mean that much to her.

But it did.

Chapter Three

"Yes, Mom," Terri said. "Of course."

Clarke paused at her office door, his hand raised to knock. She tapped her headset mic and waved him inside. She wasn't giving her mother her full attention, surfing the internet with the sound turned off while her mother talked. She had heard every story a hundred times before. She focused long enough to catch the last words of a diatribe about organic eating.

"I hate wheat germ." She thought she'd landed on a safe statement, one she made often enough that she didn't need to try and piece together what her mother said.

Her lips compressed while her mother launched into a critical examination of Terri's inability to take the discussion seriously. When her mother ranted, she realized she'd made no mention of the grain. Busted. Terri caught Clarke's suppressed amusement and grinned, clapping her fingers and thumb together in a talking sound with her free hand. She gestured to her guest chair, and he sat, sprawling in the furniture that was too small for his frame.

"Ew, you're not serious." This in response to her mother's suggestion to add raw bean sprouts to her diet. "I eat salads and limit red meat. I've got this great pineapple chicken recipe that…" The mention of both proteins brought a fresh tirade about the treatment of animals and how Terri should consider a vegetarian, or better yet, a vegan, diet. She held the phone away from her ear. "Mom."

The tirade continued, leaping to the discussion of how lambs were treated and how Terri should never eat them. The lecture was well meant, and she tried to be patient, but sometimes, like now, her tolerance was sorely tested. Still, her parents had been there for her when she shut down and redirected her life after the Clarke Affair. They knew what had happened but didn't understand why she'd given up her dreams of becoming an actress and gone back to school for her MBA. They didn't like the idea of her throwing away her dream, but in the end they had been there through the crisis. They always supported her, even if they didn't recognize the business person who had become their daughter.

"Mom," she said again. "Mom!"

Her mother stopped, something in Terri's tone no doubt alerting her that she'd gone on too long.

"I've got someone in my office. I'll call you next week. I love you." Before her mother could respond, Terri hung up the phone and turned to Clarke.

"Your mother?" His quizzical appearance was almost comical.

She picked up a pen and began pressing the clicker over and over again. "Yeah. She wanted to share a tofu recipe she'd found at the only organic store in our area. It's easier to nod and say yes. Is there something I can help you with?"

He opened his mouth and then shut it. He turned in the desk chair, drumming his fingers on the arm. "Um…" he said and trailed off.

His royal blue silk shirt was open and unbuttoned

just enough to show a bit of chest hair peeking out from under the sides of the cloth and the collar. She knew he was furry in that area, both from pictures and from personal experience.

"She can go on for hours if I let her. Thanks for the save." She tried to shake the image of his naked chest from her mind. "What's up?"

He leaned forward, his eyebrows drawn together, his forearms resting on his thighs. He shook his head. "Kai told me Jungle Ready is getting a lot of attention on microblogs, and the posts were picked up across the site."

She met his gaze. A peculiar light was in them, burning from within. That was probably just her overheated imagination.

"That's good to hear. I'll hustle for shares, ask my friends to do the same." She made a note to message Ally later. "We've got that record release party in a few days. It's great we're generating buzz. Things are tough out there. Is that all?"

He shook his head. The pensive quality to his manner left her breathless. The silence stretched out for several beats too long.

"I thought…" he said and trailed off. He moved to her desk and stood there, his arms folded.

Terri opened her mouth to speak but didn't. She stared up at him, trying to keep her face blank and not show the consternation that flowed through her veins.

"I thought you were a Type A personality who had been in a sorority, with a perfect family and two point five pets. I thought you went to church on Sunday and used to wear uniforms to school. I thought—"

He broke off when she let out a harsh sound, more

a sob than a laugh.

"A *sorority girl*? Me?" Something broke inside her, and the laughter kept coming until she forced herself to stop.

His eyes widened as he studied her. He returned to the guest chair, his fingernails scoring the arm.

"That's pretty far from the truth. No sororities allowed in my family. It's just not done. We are pretty counterculture. Down to the offbeat names."

He opened his mouth again and then turned and gestured to the nameplate outside her office. "I've been wondering what Tyris means."

She shrugged, hoping the gesture was as determinedly nonchalant as she could make it. "It doesn't mean anything other than 'something to pick on the hippie girl about' when I was in school. The origin is from the name Tyrus, which is a male name from Latin meaning 'a person from Tyre.' My parents liked the way the name sounded with our last name, and they wanted something unique. I've been Terri for as long as I can remember. My family still calls me Tyris." Her voice faded as memories trickled across her mind. "That first day of class was always a bitch. I was usually first in roll call through grade school, and the kids would always snicker when the teacher stumbled over my first name. They would chant *Tyris, Tyris* in a sing-song way." She focused on Clarke and waved her hand. "Luckily there's not much you can do to the name Tyris, or things could have been worse."

"Bad memories?" he hazarded.

"Nothing beyond the usual. We weren't bullied. My folks were vegetarians and marched to the beat of a different drummer, but they didn't make us bring weird things to school, and they kept a pretty low profile."

"Us?" His voice rose as he met her gaze.

She couldn't read his expression. "I've got two older brothers. They're back in Maine. I'm the only transplant. They tell me every time they talk to me that California will fall into the ocean after the Big One."

"I gather you weren't supposed to leave the family farm?"

"Or the commune." She strove for a casual tone.

"Damn, really? I sure as hell wouldn't have imagined you came from some free-love compound."

She acted so corporate, so proper and stiff, she imagined he couldn't reconcile her growing up in an alternative lifestyle with the silk shell and modest-skirted woman in front of him. Little did he know.

The silence grew for a moment, and she clicked the pen again. She already was aware of the answer to the question she was about to ask Clarke but wanted to listen to him tell her in that sexy tenor voice with its slight burr of whiskey.

"What about you? Where did you grow up? What about your family?"

He toyed with the arm of the guest chair again, his eyes focused away, toward the back of her monitor. "I'm still picturing you as a kid running through a patch of alfalfa, if that shit grows in Maine. Me? I've got a married younger sister and the older brother I told you about earlier—the pork council one. They have five kids between them. My sister is local. My oldest niece Sandra is..." He paused and counted off. "Fifteen, I think. Her birthday is coming up."

He met her gaze, and Terri suppressed a wince at the hint of extra moisture lurking in his eyes.

"I haven't been around any of them since my last arrest. They live down in Mission Viejo. I have to wait for them to come around, if they do. My sister and I are all right, but it's easier not to rock the boat. I did a ton of awful shit to them while high."

She opened and then shut her mouth. "I'm sorry."

"Don't be. I did it to myself. As far as education, I went to high school but not college. We formed Attraction while in high school and got our first deal a year after we hit the circuit."

"Bet you were popular. Did you play all the backyard parties?" She was such an asshole. She knew all this and yet was pasting interest on her face like she was hearing the tale for the first time.

"Oh yeah," he said with a big grin. "We had groupies, even in high school. We liked the older girls. Our favorites were the ones old enough to drive and drink. I'll never forget that first taste of alcohol. I had come home. My best friend had showed up and would never leave my side." He came to an abrupt stop, his face twisting.

His eyes changed to a deep forest green. Waving his hand in a casual gesture, he focused on her. "There's a question you want to ask. Go ahead, Tyris."

The way he drew out her name sent a bolt of sensation down her spine. She did not need this. She should find an excuse to get rid of him.

"How long have you been clean?"

He paused, his hand in the air, and studied her before letting his hand drop. "I've been sober for two years. I've been struggling to stay that way for five. In the past I would be dry for weeks and then fall off the wagon with a vengeance."

"Do you go to meetings?"

"Once or twice a week. I have trouble with that 'powerless against my addiction' stuff, so AA doesn't fit me in that way. The program is great for a lot of people. I hold myself responsible for my addiction, not God. I want to tough my cravings out, not surrender my will to a higher power. It's hard to reconcile that with what AA teaches, but I muddle through. I work an okay program, not a great one."

"That's admirable."

He appeared startled but then smiled. "Thanks. I could do a lot more."

"We all could. That's how life works. There's always something to be done."

He gestured around the office. "The way I hear it, you do everything that needs doing around here, so I'm not sure that's true."

She had no way to tell him the truth. No way to tell him that the obsessive child she had been grew up and learned to channel her energy into productive work, leaving her no time to woolgather over the impossible. The way she behaved in the past still filled her with shame. Terri tried not to focus on that. Work she could do. Recipes she could break down. If she had a problem, she would figure it out for herself. Never again would she be the person that others rolled their eyes at behind her back. She would not obsess over a man, not drive her friends crazy with endless questions about *did he look at me just now* and other nonsense. It would not happen again.

"Thanks, but don't compliment me. I'm doing what needs doing." She clenched her jaw, willing him to stop. So much danced on the end of her tongue that she clamped her teeth over it. The truth slid through her consciousness—an unwelcome reminder of the past.

A combination of hurt and resignation crossed Clarke's face. He gripped the guest chair and then hauled himself out of it. His face shut down by inches until all that was left was something that might have been called disinterested, if she didn't know him so well. Something primal blazed out from behind his eyes, but he said nothing.

She couldn't tell him the truth. Once he was reminded of who she was—Lynx the little Maine stalker—he would never feel the same way about her again. He would feel about her the way she did about her past self—shame and horror. No point in saying anything. He didn't recognize her, and she was sure as hell going to keep it that way.

"I'll leave you to it." He raised a hand. "See you at the club on Tuesday?"

She nodded, feeling like she had just let something important slip away. "You will. I'm handling the arrangements."

"Of course you are."

****

Clarke paced around his apartment, trying to stay away from his phone. It beckoned to him like a lifeline, promising him a respite from this empty feeling inside him.

He had women he could call. Even now, with his life in tatters, plenty of women would gladly come over if he asked. It would be nothing to pick up the phone and get one of them. Although he'd deleted his contacts after he got out of rehab, a number had slid back into his contact list. Many, if not all, of them would be happy to go out on a date…and beyond.

He should do that. His body ached for fulfillment, for the feeling of another person's warmth against his as he brought both of them to the edge and over. It would be child's play. Hell, he could go to a meeting— the directory held plenty of meetings specializing in musicians. Additionally, many people went to meetings for the wrong reasons. It would be nothing to get a woman.

No. He didn't want *a* woman. His perverse freaking body had betrayed him. It wanted *one* woman. One infuriating, insulting, annoying woman with red-gold hair and eyes the color of a summer storm.

Behaving in such a manner was a dangerous slope. He could lust after a woman he couldn't have and use it as an excuse to dip back into other bad behaviors. He should stick to what was in front of him, taking life day by day and doing the best he could with the time. ODAT—one day at a time—was his sponsor's favorite phrase. What he should not be doing was imagining how Terri would be like out on a date, holding hands and gazing at him with approval and longing. He should not be picturing what it would be like to go on a picnic with her, or to the beach, or a freaking bike ride, and share moments with her. He should not be thinking about what his family would think of a woman like her, so different from the models and actresses he inflicted on them in his rock-star days. That was so unlikely that it might as well have been fiction. He needed to stick the entire concept in the bucket called "shit that will never happen, starring people who will never be in your life."

That's what he should do. What he wanted to do

was get Terri's number from Kai and call her, which was insanity. He had added her on his social media, and she him, but that had been a work thing. Despite himself, he went to her profile now, scrolling through her feed and at the few pictures she posted. Terri's profile was like the woman, private, careful, and stingy with details. Her posts were related to work events and recipes—lots and lots of recipes.

One person jumped out at him. He recognized the name Ally Wilson from the band days. She had dated Harris, his former bass player, for a while if he was not mistaken. It reinforced what Kai had said earlier about Terri going to the local clubs when she first came to town. She could have met Ally there. If Ally and Terri had ever hung together at the clubs, he had no memory of it. He had not ever encountered Terri on the local club scene "back in the day," or he would have remembered it. Her striking red-gold hair was unusual, and it would have stood out. He would have taken note of her, even if she couldn't stand up against the gorgeous women who infested their lives at that time.

Wouldn't he?

He cursed himself for an idiot and closed the browser. Speculating about Terri would do no good. She wasn't interested in getting to know him. She'd made that abundantly clear, even if her sentences didn't come with the same scorn that they had when they were first introduced.

Checking the meeting schedule online, he took note of an upcoming meeting and left the house. He had to do something, or he might do something he regretted.

He wasn't sure which of the several options was the most foolish.

Chapter Four

Terri's gaze moved around the club, cataloging its contents. A catered buffet lined one wall, with plastic cups shaped like wine glasses stacked there and throughout the room. Tip jars were placed in prominent locations. A hired bartender stood behind the beer and wine bar, thumbing through his phone. Banners with the band name hung above the platform, with the Jungle Ready band website as well as the record label URL in the opposite corners. The equipment was all on stage and ready for the night's activities. Everything was a little shabby in the bright light, like a set of clothes tailored once too often.

She consulted her checklist again. All the boxes were ticked off, but she went through them one more time. The sound system was being tested, and she listened to the low notes to ensure they were calibrated properly.

A figure blocked the doorway before stepping inside. The light behind the man poured through the room, silhouetting him in yellow slices of sunlight and dust motes for a moment before he shut the door behind him.

Clarke crossed the room to her, his gaze never leaving hers. A quiver of excitement shot through her, racing along her bloodstream. She swallowed down her anxiety, her throat dry, and watched him until he was close enough to speak.

"Hi," he said in that husky voice that made her nerve endings tingle.

"Hi yourself. Here to check on things?"

His gaze went to the buffet spread. Terri eyed the chicken wings, sausage rolls, and chips and dips with a critical eye before turning to him.

"Something like that." He pointed to the buffet. "You could have done better, right?" His eloquent look told her he was already aware of the answer.

She gave him a tired nod. "Of course. There are many interesting things I could have done. But Kai vetoed it. He said I was stretched too thin." She glanced at the spread again, and then, like iron drawn to a magnet, her gaze went back to Clarke.

"Smart man. Kai is delayed, so he sent me down to see if you needed anything." His glance took in the room again. "It appears you have everything well in hand. As usual."

Using her clipboard as a shield, she pretended to be examining its contents. The clipboard was better than meeting that green gaze and wondering how his eyes would change when he was inside her. "I think I'm good. Are you going to be okay? You know, in a club?" Heat flooded her. Her lovers through the years had been fine, but sex was ordinary. She had never again experienced the electricity race through her blood the way it did when she was around Clarke.

"With all the temptation around me, you mean?" He gestured to where the bartender was now wiping down the counter.

She was glad the dim club concealed the heat that crawled up her cheeks. "Yeah."

"I have to live my life, Tyris. That means I have to be strong enough to go to a club and not drink. I'm far enough into my sobriety that I can handle being around alcohol." He grinned, but the gesture ended somewhere around his cheekbones. "Kai hired me to do A&R and generate press. That involves clubs."

"That's got to be tough."

A flicker of amusement and something primal danced in his eyes before his gaze slid to the floor. "If I get triggered, there's a midnight meeting nearby. This is my job. Anything I can do to help?" He stopped, and she turned the clipboard with all its boxes checked toward him. He grunted out a short bark of laughter. "Of course it's done. Let's go and get some coffee, clear out of here. You need a break."

She chewed on her lower lip for a minute. "Just for a few." She reached for her purse. "You are right. I need to get away from here."

After leaving her cell phone number with the bartender in case of an emergency, Terri followed Clarke out into the afternoon sunshine.

He fell into step with her, maneuvering so he was on the outside of the sidewalk. He pointed to a little coffee shop down the busy street a few doors from where the event was taking place.

She yawned.

His eyebrows furrowed at the motion. "You work too hard."

"Someone has to. Kai's job is to try to keep the label from going under. He has to deal with investors and sweet talk people. Yours is to find bands and promote the crap out of us online. Mine is to keep the label's gears running. Overtime comes with the territory."

"It shouldn't be your life."

"It is what it is." She glanced at the cars waiting at a red light. *What life,* she wanted to say.

He took her elbow and guided her into the restaurant.

"You're not a one woman show," he said once they were seated. "Other employees work here too."

Behind them the roar of the early stages of rush hour could be heard on the street, echoing off the buildings and bouncing into the café. A waitress with a pencil behind her ear approached them. She had on a starchy uniform, a throwback to lunch ladies and fifties diners. Her spectacles were on a thick chain and stuck haphazardly on her hairnet-covered up-do.

"Whatchawant?" She set two glasses of water down with a clunk. Ice clouded the etched glass, coating the outside with condensation.

Terri suppressed a giggle, the near caricature almost making her break out into inappropriate laughter. She needed to get some sleep.

"Two coffees," Clarke said after a glance at her. "Is your club sandwich good?" He motioned at the board that announced it as today's offering. The chalk was smudged, the selection rarely changed.

The waitress made an indeterminate gesture with her pen. "It works."

Before Terri could open her mouth, Clarke handed the menus back and nodded. "Two specials."

"There's no need to spend money. The buffet." She waved toward the club.

"Once the party starts, you and that clipboard will be too busy running around to remember to put food in your system. Besides, I saw the way you examined that buffet. I doubt you want anything they have to offer. Eat something. You'll burn it off. Not that you need to lose weight."

She opened her mouth, intending to say something caustic about supermodels and wafer-thin women. Then she clamped her jaw shut. Anything she said would be unkind. Not knowing what else to do, Terri nodded. The server heaved her bulk kitchenward, leaving the faint scent of Jean Nate in her wake.

Clarke's eyes hooded before he turned his attention toward the rushing traffic on the street near their café. Across the way thrift stores and general shops bustled with activity. The discount store nearby was bursting with customers. People honked at the cars in front of them as others jockeyed for parking spaces or turned down side streets, hoping for a break in traffic.

"Attraction's last record release party was at a club in Hollywood," he said. "Huge affair. The guest list was the 'in' thing to be on. The label went all out. All I had to do was roll out of my place and down the hill. I got there, somehow. I was at home, drinking my ass off beforehand."

She remembered the incident and the glee that washed through her when he was derided in the news. The incident had come as a surprise to nobody. Clarke had been so late people had begun leaving, and was a drunken mess when he did show up. He had barely been able to get through the short set, stumbling around and slurring the lyrics. At least he'd been there. At that point in his career, his reliability was very much in question.

"I heard. Do you still have the place?" She knew

all too well the home he had taken her that night. She figured he'd lost the townhouse and all his other possessions when everything went sour.

The waitress came back, setting mugs of steaming coffee down on the table with a thud. She turned and left, meandering over to the only other occupied table in the café.

"Yeah." He grinned, his face lighting up with the movement.

"That's remarkable."

This new Clarke made her heart stop in a different way than it had when she was a girl. The younger man had nothing on this guy. This one had a few signs of age, but he was far more interesting than the wild rock star whose antics tore up the gossip columns.

"I paid cash for that place and the one in Glendale. Real estate is freedom. There's nothing, well, almost nothing in this world to compare."

She would regret asking but did anyway. "What tops it?"

He shot her a glance full of hidden meaning and shades of innuendo. It promised things her run-of-the-mill sexual experiences couldn't fulfill. She was efficient and smart and got the job done but lacked that alluring quality other women had that kept male fascination alive. She wasn't the type men went gaga for. No point in mourning what she would never have.

"Have you ever been in love?"

She blinked, terror surging through her. He would have no way of understanding what a loaded question he'd asked. He had no memory of their one and only night, just like he had no memories of many other one-night stands. Granted, not many of those other women harassed him until he threatened legal action, but he didn't remember that either. The only cost for her to answer was pride.

"I thought I was, once." She prayed the words didn't show their hidden meaning. Unable to meet the vivid sea green of his eyes, she focused on the street.

"What happened?" he asked, touching her hand with his fingers. He started and drew back his hand, folding his fingers around his palm. Taking a sip of his coffee, he glanced anywhere but at her.

Heat pulsed through her hand at the simple touch, and sensation shot across her nerve endings. She resisted the urge to rub the back of her hand on her denim-clad legs to rid herself of the bolt of awareness.

"I meant nothing to him." She tried to keep her voice level. He had no idea what that effort cost her. "I was young and inexperienced, and he was worldly and out of my league. He wanted sex and that was all. I kidded myself that he could be talked into a relationship, but I knew, deep down, what I was getting into. I should have known better. I don't want to talk about it." She picked up her water glass, playing with the top before drinking.

He opened his mouth as though he was going to protest but then nodded, his Adam's apple convulsing on a hard swallow. "All right. Change of subject. Tyris August, what do you do for fun?"

She coughed and choked on a piece of ice. She set the suddenly slippery glass down. "I get out." Even to her, the words sounded hollow and unconvincing.

"Doing what?"

Good question. She reviewed her non-work activities. One time she'd gone to the Getty with Sheila.

That was…oh heck, a year ago. Then she went bike riding with Yvonne and David…and it had been four months since she'd done that. Cooking was pleasurable but also a passion rather than recreation. Her life was a blur of work and basic house chores. She had Ally, of course, and they got together every few weeks. Their activities primarily centered around hiking and the occasional lunch date on a weekend. Lately, though, Ally had been distracted. She'd mentioned something about a "Dirk" starting at the office. Terri made a mental note to call Ally and plan an activity.

"You know what?" She picked up her coffee mug and downed the remains before setting it on the table with a thud. "You're right. I don't have fun. There's no time in my life for nonsense." All she could think about was the sleek hardness of the muscles she glimpsed under his shirts and pants and what they would feel like against her skin.

"That can change."

Part of her wanted to lash out at him, tell him to get the hell out of her life, and storm off. She paused, almost reaching for her purse to exit in a grand gesture. As the silence lengthened, his face sank, and a shadowed pain hollowed his eyes.

He studied her for a moment and then shook his head. "None of my business. I get it."

She wanted to touch him again, to slide her hand over his until their fingers interlaced. The compulsion was stronger than any she'd ever felt toward a man, even Clarke, back in the day. "It's not *not* your business."

He grinned at the purposeful double negative.

"It's been a long time since I let myself have fun. I

don't have any idea how to change, or even if I want to." She turned a bright grin on him, hoping to erase the dark shadows under his skin.

"It might be a good idea to try, though."

****

I meant nothing to him.

Clarke watched the band perform, even as his mind was a riot of tumbled emotions. Live, Jungle Ready was as talented as the CD. Their notes were clean and on pitch. The guys thrashed around the stage, moshing on the raised wood and throwing their long hair around in every way possible.

He watched Terri whenever her attention was directed elsewhere and she wouldn't notice. As he had suspected, once they got back to the club, she became one with the clipboard. She didn't eat or drink or do anything except run from place to place.

He had to clench his hands to stop from forcing a glass of water or some finger food into her closed fists. She'd made it clear she had this under control and didn't need his assistance.

I don't have fun.

The party had had a good turnout, and almost all the fifty people Terri invited showed up. A handful of critics were present who had been selected for their musical preferences.

The noise was at almost deafening decibels, and he was grateful for the custom-made earplugs he'd owned for years, bought when they toured two hundred days a year. He was sure they had saved him from too-early hearing loss.

Considering how loaded he'd been all the time, he was surprised how much he'd been able to do while plastered off his ass. Days, even weeks, were lost to his memory. At the end there had been no hiding from the addiction.

In all that time, he hadn't lived. He'd run from everything, his mental state, his career, his life. Sex was one of the only pleasures he'd had left. Alcohol and coke had numbed him to feeling any other emotions. In the end he'd used sex as a way to feel alive. If he were honest with himself, he'd used sex for many other things except the one that mattered—to show a woman he loved her.

That was the worst thing about rehab. The feelings. Everything was brighter, louder, and more intense as the days passed and the drugs were flushed from his system. Sometimes he felt like screaming, others crying, emotions battering at the doors of his conscious brain for the first time in over fifteen years.

Eventually he came to terms with the riot of sensations. Instead of drugs he lost himself in painting and refocused his life to one of sobriety. He had always assumed he could quit, but the constant relapses told him otherwise. The twelve-step programs he'd had to attend were hard. The cognitive behavioral therapy that went along with his program helped him get his animal brain into perspective. He was only one drink or line away from disaster at any time.

He glanced at Terri again, bustling around, dealing with the caterers and the bartenders and the merchandise people. She pampered the industry folks, making sure they were well taken care of. Her hair was clipped back as always, but tendrils of the curly red-blond mass had escaped the barrette and were lying, damp, against her forehead and cheeks. It would be so sweet to tear that clip off and bury his hands into those tresses. He wanted to press his fingers to her scalp until her head tilted up to him and her lips parted for his kiss.

The only explanation was that he had gone insane. He had to be crazy to think she saw him as anything other than an addict. At best he was a co-worker she hadn't wanted, an unwelcome intruder who took up time and energy she could use for other things.

He could take on additional tasks, which was part of the reason he had convinced Kai to let him deal with the event tonight. He wanted to be useful and not the burden he had too often been. If the amends started with a woman he had never met, then he was okay with that. He could give her someone to rely on, and pay his enormous debt forward.

He had hoped some of the gossip bloggers would turn up, but none were in evidence. The best he could hope for was personal pictures or some quick messages. He could post on his own microblogging account and try to get a couple of the kids there to do the same. Perhaps one of them would go viral and get picked up by other bloggers. He'd write his own blog. He'd put some pictures out there and ask for likes. He still had some clout with fans.

The band finished their brief set, and Clarke breathed a sigh of relief, his ears taking a minute to adjust to the quiet. He was getting too old for this shit.

He spotted Terri again, and to his surprise she was motioning to him. He yanked out his ear plugs, striding through the thinning crowd to the side of the club. A few people stopped him on the way, and he posed for pictures, smiling and signing autographs before moving on to the next. He gave her a glance and then peered toward backstage. Clarke dealt with people as swiftly as possible, feeling the pressure of her impatient glances. He shook his head, gave the last person a brisk nod, and moved to Terri.

"Can you help with the signings?" She pointed to a table that was set up with merchandise. "I can't locate the singer. I have to find him." She sounded frantic and a little desperate.

His eyebrows lifted. "I'm on it." The guitar player came through the door behind her. He glimpsed two other people in the shadows of the backstage entrance, coming toward him.

One guy Clarke pegged as the drummer stopped, his eyes growing large. "Clarke Masters," he said and offered his hand. "I'm Jeff. You led a meeting once at my sober living. Great message, man. I've been clean for…" He trailed off, glancing at Terri.

Anonymity, the hallmark of all twelve-step programs, was only as good as the people keeping others' information private. He was candid about his sobriety, but not everyone was.

He took the offered hand and shook firmly. "How long?"

Terri disappeared into the backstage area, her gaze darting first to Jeff and then back to Clarke before she left. Her hair was coming loose from the clip, hanging in messy clumps around her face.

"Four months. A hundred and twenty-seven days."

"That's great, man. Congratulations. All we've got is today."

Jeff gripped Clarke's hand too tightly. "Thanks, dude. It's tough. I think about drinking all the time."

Clarke paused for a second and then took out his

thin wallet, retrieving a card. He had made them up in early sobriety at the suggestion of his sponsor, to hand out to people in meetings. He had been fearful of giving his number out, but to his surprise they were rarely used.

Then again, he remembered getting numbers in his first days and throwing them away. Sometimes he threw them out of his car window as he drove from the meeting. In theory collecting numbers sounded good. As a member of AA, he could reach out to a fellow alcoholic if he was in trouble. In reality, if he wanted to drink, no amount of numbers was going to stop him.

"Call me anytime." He pressed the card in the drummer's palm, his hand over the other man's. "Sobriety is possible."

Terri reappeared. She seemed to want to say something but remained quiet. Jeff flushed and stepped back, wiping his hand on his dirty jeans and slipping the card into his back pocket. He put his head down.

"They're signing," she said after a long pause.

"Go for it." Clarke pushed Jeff toward the door. "This is your moment."

Jeff nodded and disappeared into the main part of the club.

Terri shut the door, and the chatter of people eased. The muscles in her neck worked. She pushed a hand across her head. Her weariness was apparent in the slow motion.

"Everything okay?"

"I'm good."

He stepped to her, taking in her drained posture and the circles under her eyes. "Are you done? You should clear out."

She made a vague gesture to the front area. "I need to stay…"

He moved closer to her and gripped her shoulders. He could tell it wouldn't be long before exhaustion won out over determination. "Go home. I'll watch over things and lock up. Go. I can come in late tomorrow. I'm sure you will be there to do all the zillion things you juggle."

That got a smile from her, if only a wan one. "Not that many. Maybe a hundred million. I'm going to take you up on that." She handed him a satchel. "If you need anything, my number is in there."

He was still touching her. The heat and subtle fragrance of her sent hunger surging through him. To his surprise, she didn't move, neither retreating nor stepping into him. Need seared across his nerve endings. The longing to feel her was almost overwhelming.

Acting on the desire to push her into the wall and kiss her until she responded would be a bad idea. The animal part of him lurched forward, fighting with the rational side, telling him to do it anyway.

"Good night, Terri." He bent down and grazed his lips over hers before drawing her into him in what he hoped was a gentle hug. All he wanted to do was curve his hands down her body and arch her pelvis into his, letting her feel his hard length. Her arms stayed still for a moment and then went around his body, sliding over his neck and pressing against the top of his spine. Her breath exhaled against his ear, and his lust intensified.

If she realized how she was affecting him, she would run. With a reluctant sigh, he released her and stepped back.

Her eyes were huge, her breathing rougher than it had been a minute ago. Maybe she was more aware of him as a man than she let on.

"Go home. I'll see you tomorrow."

Terri nodded and swallowed again. To his delight, she took in a ragged breath as if his nearness was impacting her like it had crashed through him.

"Good night," she murmured before she slipped away.

Chapter Five

"Eight o'clock." Clarke caught sight of Terri and motioned her into his office as he spoke. "Yeah, that's right, Gigantor. Great. Sure. Friday, sounds good."

He hung up, meeting her gaze. He glanced at the tickets in his free hand before focusing his attention on her.

Gigantor was the biggest local sensation to come out of Los Angeles in years. Their retro sound, harkening back to Guns N' Roses and Van Halen, was right up Clarke's alley. They were gaining a following every day. Gigantor was a band ripe to be signed. An online video they'd put out had gone viral, and lots of labels were sniffing around. She doubted Apposite had much of a chance of attracting the hot band's attention.

"What's this?" She tried to keep her voice casual, but the jealous thread in her tone was obvious. "A date?"

A smile played over his lips. "Yeah. Friend of Bill. She's a model. Her name is…" He paused a moment and rummaged on his desk until he found a business card. "Ariana Blank. She needs friends."

A wave of pure, fierce jealousy streaked through her abdomen. Models. Of course his date would be a model. She mulled over who "Bill" was, until she remembered that was the phrase many AA people used as shorthand for a member of their group.

"Ariana." She turned the name over in her mind, gripped with a desire to rip the unknown woman in half. And of course she was an alcoholic, or an addict, or whatever. She probably was a gorgeous drunk. Well, she wouldn't be so pretty if Terri took her apart, would she?

Without speaking, she took out her smartphone and found Ariana Blank. The woman didn't have much of a resume, with just a few credits, but she made up for that with plenty of photos. She had the usual model appearance, quintessentially Los Angeles. Her profile said she was six feet tall. She had short blond hair, long legs, and weighed about a pound and a half.

Terri thumbed the shutdown button so she didn't have to stare at the striking face. "Have fun." She tossed some local magazines down on his desk. "Kai thought there might be some interesting underground bands in here for you to check out. He dog-eared a few pages."

She tried to ignore the sinking feeling of despair that coursed through her. She had imagined his razor-sharp focus when he was around her. She had nothing to offer a former rock star. She had nothing to give to any man, especially not the man who had called her a stalker. Why her stupid body and mind had chosen this one, of all men, to continue to be fascinated by was a question she had no answer to. He hadn't been the only man who found her boring in bed. Others over the years had made their feelings clear. She had no allures to keep the opposite sex around for the long haul. Focusing on work was rewarding. She was good at that. Focusing on what could not be was idiotic.

She remembered the first time she had gotten

involved with someone after Clarke. She was still reeling from the experience but determined to get on with her life. The poor man's name was Dino, and he had been infatuated with her from the first time they were introduced. She ignored his advances until the Clarke thing imploded, then accepted a date the next time he asked. He was a nice guy who didn't deserve a still-raw, traumatized Terri. No matter how hard she tried and told herself she should like this guy, she wasn't able to get past how she felt about Clarke. Dino tried, and failed, to breach the walls she hastily erected around herself. It was the first time she faked an orgasm in bed, but it hadn't been the last. She was sure that she had not been kind to him, but that memory was fortunately faded. Dino had been a nice guy and not said anything, but she had disappointed him in bed. It wouldn't be the last time for that either.

"Hey, you okay?"

"Sure!" She conjured up a wide-eyed appearance. "Just thought you'd want these." She waved to the cheaply produced local papers. The memories that were surfacing were intense and too painful to deal with right now. She had to get out. "Well, duty calls. Got to go. Bye."

****

Clarke stared at the spot where she had been standing even after her scent vanished from the air. He didn't move. Minutes passed. He had imagined the hurt in her eyes. No way was the cool, collected, self-contained Terri August bothered by the idea of him going out on a date.

Still…

For one brief second he'd glimpsed a shadow of

jealousy before she masked it by the too-wide eyes.

He threw down his pen, which bounced on his desk before landing next to his keyboard. He picked up the scattered papers with his other hand. He thumbed through them, taking note of the bands Kai had circled, some with a question mark, some with an exclamation point. They could do all the same things online, but both Kai and Clarke liked the feel of newsprint.

Minutes passed.

He should stay in his office and focus on work. He should remember that a little over a month ago she had examined him like something she wouldn't take the time to scrape off her shoe. Her feelings could not have changed in such a short period.

He rose from his desk and shoved his chair into the open slot. *Fuck it*. He'd been shot down plenty of times in the past several years. Terri's denial shouldn't bruise his ego beyond what any others had. If he was going to be the new, improved Clarke, he had to be honest with his feelings.

He walked out the open door and into the office space. No, he couldn't lie to himself. Being rejected by her was different. The contempt in her eyes and the scathing comments she'd made at the beginning still stung.

He greeted the mailroom kid, making small talk about the guy's garage band and hopes for the future while his mind drifted. Her door was open, and the lights were on, but that was no surprise. Even though she had a west-facing exposure and got plenty of natural light in the afternoon, she always had her office overheads on.

After what he hoped was a decent interval, he

made his escape from the mailroom kid and went to Terri's office. He leaned against her door, trying for an easy posture. He crossed his arms and placed his left shoulder against the molding, one leg thrust forward.

"Why do you have so many lights on?"

Clearly startled by his voice, Terri met his gaze.

She was wearing reading glasses. Every fantasy about every teacher he'd ever had surfaced in his mind and between his legs. Blood pooled heavy in his groin, and he was in danger of losing brain cells, judging by the savage intensity of his hardening member. He wanted to kiss her with her glasses on, watching her eyes go myopic as he drew closer.

Turning his body so he was in profile to her, he crossed one leg over the other, masking the distortion of his trousers.

Her hair was down. His fantasies had nothing on the reality of the thick, wavy mass. The curls fell into place in long, sweeping layers along the side of her head and a quarter of the way down her back.

He didn't move. He didn't dare. As he watched, she snatched off the glasses and tossed them to the desk. In a continuation of the same movement, she reached for the clip, which was lying on its side on a stack of magazines similar to the ones she'd given him earlier.

"No." He swallowed, trying to get some moisture into his mouth. "Please don't. Your hair...it's gorgeous."

She said nothing but let her hand drop, leaving the barrette on the desk. Marking a spot on a giant handwritten sheet she had been inputting into Excel, Terri turned her attention to Clarke.

"I'm interrupting." He should turn around and leave and let her work. "What are you doing?"

He watched as her attention went from him to the spreadsheet and then back again. "Comparisons between the adds our artists are getting and those of the major labels. We're peanuts compared to them, but some of our guys are holding their own. Mostly the ones who are good at promoting the hell out of themselves online, like Jungle Ready. My guess is most of those bands will drop us and go out on their own soon." She reached for the hair clip again but stopped. Instead she clasped her arms over one another and leaned back in her chair. He remembered the look of a few moments ago and marveled that she'd been able to put herself back together so quickly. Or perhaps he'd been imagining the hurt that momentarily dashed across her face.

Her thumbs were moving across each other in a nervous gesture partially hidden by her desk. She must think he couldn't see them. That gave him the courage to go on.

He gestured to their shared secretary. The fiftyish woman was bent to her computer, also wearing reading glasses and in the middle of something. With her privacy screen she could have been playing cards, but he didn't think so. She focused on them at Clarke's gesture, her head cocked to one side, her silent code to find out if he needed anything. At the negative shake of his head, she turned back to her computer and once again began typing.

"I don't need her, but you insist she split her time between us. You should use her. She's a workhorse." He turned and closed the door, cutting off the sounds in the office beyond.

She raised an eyebrow at his movement but made no protest. "Sunshine is for both of us. There's a lot you can do with her. Did you need something? I gave you all the magazines. If there's something you're missing, tell me. Or you can go online…"

With a growl, he moved from his spot against the door. "I can get my own stuff," he said in a sharp, staccato tone. "From now on why don't you let me get the magazines? Save you a trip. If you don't need copies, I'll just get them for myself."

Her gaze darted from the door and back to him. Her irises widened as if she were frightened. He wanted to crowd her and forced himself to stop at the back of her desk. Her gaze slid past him, avoiding his eyes.

"That's not part of your job description," she said, a quaver in her tone. Her smooth, pink tongue darted out and played over the middle of her lips before retreating back inside that luscious mouth.

He gripped the edge with hands like claws, hoping she mistook the action for firmness and not the jolt of lust that surged through his veins. *What the hell.* He stepped back, his arousal delineated against the zipper of his pants.

"My job description is fluid. I can do whatever you need me to." He crossed his arms and prayed his voice didn't shake from need. "Including getting your magazines if that's what you want. You work too hard. Let me lend a hand."

"Um…" Her gaze fell to his crotch and then back up into his eyes. "Er…you're not thinking…I need help in that way, are you?"

If he weren't so aroused, he would have laughed.

"No, not unless you wanted to." At her terrified air his smile faded. "Don't worry, that's not my style. Not these days, anyway. You're safe with me."

She choked out a word that might have been on a laugh or a cry. "Safe is an interesting word. I'll accept it."

"Trust me. I know when I'm beat. I don't have a snowball's chance in hell with you," he said in a throaty tone, placing his hands on her desk and leaning over. "I'm not stupid. I have no chance with you."

****

She swallowed, her hands playing across her curly mane. It had been unwise of her to take the hair clip out. Clipped, her hair spoke of discipline, order, direction. She'd been told her unbound curls resembled a gypsy's hair, full of mystery and magic. They promised hot sex and wild abandon between the sheets. Told of dark nights of passion, sweaty bodies and desire, fantasies fulfilled between two consenting parties. She was sorry he had seen her with her hair down. He might expect things she'd learned from grim sexual experience she wasn't able to fulfill. She had been able to compose herself, but him in her closed office was playing havoc with all her good intentions.

"My...lights," she said.

"What?"

Clarke's hands were still on her desk. His formidable erection pressed against his pants. His hard length made the fly separate until the serrated edges of the zipper were visible against the cloth. He sat down, landing so heavily into her guest chair that the wood squeaked.

"My lights." She met the vivid green of his eyes.

"Lights?" he repeated in a distracted tone.

"You asked why I liked my lights so bright." She was pleased with how even her voice was. "I need reading glasses. They help minimize that."

She had no idea how she was able to manage intelligent conversation. The need to touch him was overwhelming. Only the smooth oak of the desk separating them kept her from putting her hand on his arm. She had been attracted to her share of men since her ridiculous crush on Clarke, but not like this. Never like him. A part of her was thrilled that she could feel, if only lust. The emotion brought alive something she'd assumed was dormant or gone.

"Oh." He blinked as he focused on her again. He crossed one leg over the other, a motion that hid his impressive erection. She was sorry for that. At least women didn't have their desire show so plainly. Still, the idea that he found her sexy sent a thrill through her nerve endings. Arousal began deep in her body, hardening her nipples and moistening her underwear.

"What can I do for you?" She steepled her fingers into a V in an attempt to conceal how much they were trembling.

His gaze took in the abstract posters on her wall, the purse resting against her bookshelf, and the beige throw rug under his feet before his gaze met hers again. "Go out with me Friday. I'll cancel with Ariana."

She gaped at him, her mouth dropping open into what she was sure was a very unattractive, rounded O. "Be serious. Thanks, but that goes above and beyond." She ignored the obvious indication of his arousal.

"What?" His brow furrowed as he studied her.

"Duty and all that. I admitted I don't get out much.

You shouldn't feel like you single-handedly will change that." Inwardly, she applauded herself. She sounded rational and normal, not the fluttering bundle of nerves inside her. Not like his "little Maine stalker." He hadn't even commented on her blatant change of topic, despite its incredible lack of subtlety.

Terri released her hands from the steeple position. What she wanted to do was push through her hair and pretend his hands were there, burying his long fingers into the mass while he held her head still for a deep, thrusting French kiss.

"That's not...damn it." He propelled himself up and began pacing back and forth in front of her desk. Finally, he stopped in front of her.

Frightened by the predatory intensity of his gaze, she drew back, moving her chair until the wheels hit the credenza behind her. The action pushed her body into view, exposing her to his gaze. His eyes went to her legs.

Sure she wouldn't meet the standards of the super model he had a date with, she let him drink in his fill.

Clarke had always chosen models and strippers, and to think he'd changed his preferences was madness. The fact that he was aroused right now didn't matter. That happened to men sometimes.

"You're beautiful," he said.

She laughed, the noise a harsh bark. Perhaps in Maine she would be pretty, but in Hollywood she was average. She'd learned that lesson well over the years.

He came around the desk, crowding her against the furniture. With his hands on the chair arms, he gazed deep into her eyes. His head was so close to her own that if she moved even a fraction, their lips would meet.

"Please. You don't need to butter me up. We work together, remember? We can be friends, but I have no illusions that I'm the most gorgeous thing you've ever come across."

He drew back again but stayed where he was. "You're not."

Her forehead wrinkled. She had expected empty flattery, not brutal honesty. The candor should have stung, but the blunt truth was a comfort. He'd said it in a brusque tone, no falseness behind his words.

"No question the best looking woman I ever met was Maxie Butts. Butts were her, uh, specialty. She could suck the chrome off a trailer hitch, and man, she was stacked. She had the face of an angel and a body made for sin. So many curves... She was so beautiful even the sun shone brighter around her."

He paused and then grinned, a private smirk. She had seen versions of that expression dozens of times, but as with his other smiles these days, this one was real.

"She was dumb as a post and treacherous to boot, but she was stunning. She stuck with me for a while but then threw me over for the producer of my solo album. They took me for any royalties I was due. At that point I had very little to embezzle. My one satisfaction in all of that was she wasted her time. She told me I was a washed-up addict and to get my ass into rehab." He sighed and met her gaze again. "She was right about that, even if she had an IQ that didn't reach room temperature."

Terri put a hand on top of his. His skin was warm and dry. "That which does not kill you," she quoted. "One of Kai's favorite phrases."

Clarke grinned again and laced his fingers with hers. When she offered no protest, he lifted her hand off the chair and placed a kiss on the inside of her palm.

"He stole it from me," he said with a glint in his eyes. Rising, he urged her to her feet, and she didn't fight him. Her body was languid, boneless; the rational part of her mind that was screaming for her to slap him and flee was no match against the desire flooding her body.

Only this man had ever made her feel that way. Pursuing this would be a disaster. Experience had proven that. The knowledge didn't stop her from swaying toward him.

"Come with me." He put his arms around her and hauled her into him. "I don't want to go with the supermodel. I'd much rather go with you. Going to the Rumble together would be fun. Kai tells me you used to party at the clubs, but I bet you haven't been there in years. Unless you went there for work."

His hard body and the play of his muscles as he shifted to bring their bodies closer together was like coming home. She slipped her arms around him and laid her head against his chest. He made a startled sound, and then his grip tightened until she lost the ability to breathe. He brushed his lips across the top of her head.

She would not go there. She wouldn't. She knew what would happen if she did. He would kiss her, and the world would go to hell.

Aware she had a hungry, needy expression on her face, Terri tilted her head up to meet his gaze.

Clarke bent his head and fitted his mouth to hers.

The world exploded. At the touch of his lips, she

gave over to sensation, feeling him in every pore of her.

With a whimper, she curved her hands around his shoulders. His arms tightened at her back and then moved down to cup her ass and yank her into the taut evidence of his desire.

Then he was kissing her, dipping inside her mouth as his hands moved over her behind, her upper thighs, and the indentation at the small of her back. He feasted on her as he caressed her. His hips kept time with his tongue, thrusting against her soft form. She whimpered as he continued to plunder her senses with his overwhelming maleness.

He drew back. He was breathing hard and fast, his face reddened and his chest heaving. Only a slight sliver of green was visible against his dilated black pupils.

She was having trouble catching her breath. Her hair was tangled from his embrace, and her clothes were probably turned inside out by the scorching oblivion of his kiss.

"Come with me," he urged. "Screw Ariana. I want to take you."

She was somehow able to ease out of his arms, shaking her head as she did so. "I can't, Clarke. I just can't."

Chapter Six

Night drew to an inky blackness cut by the neon lights of the city streets. The sounds of rush hour wound down, the street roar dying away as commuters made their way to their next destination.

Terri focused on balancing the online banking statement to the expenses in her database. Juggling the numbers didn't change reality. Their line of credit was dangerously low, and soon there would be nothing left to draw on. They were going to need something soon.

If a group or a song didn't break out, Apposite was out of time. Stretching, she groaned as her tense shoulder muscles protested her movement. The computer clock took a minute to swim into focus, and she started with surprise at the time. After eight o'clock. On a Friday. Once again she'd let work take priority over anything social. Not that she had anything to go home to—or to do. Her few friends rarely called her, having given up at luring the reluctant woman out of her home. Maybe she should get two cats, something to keep her company. She debated calling Ally and then remembered the guy Ally had mentioned but couldn't recall his name. Something one-syllable. She was probably spending time with whatshisname. Better not to risk it. Ally was sure to figure out something was wrong if Terri called out of the blue after eight on a Friday.

Claire Davon

A sound came from the hallway, and her heart sped up at the unexpected noise. She hadn't noticed the place was deserted until the click of the front door releasing its lock filled the area.

"Who's there?" She searched for something to defend herself. The laptops were locked to the desk, but plenty of portable items were easy pickings. The motion sensor lights came on, but she couldn't determine who was there. She jumped up from her desk, not wanting to be trapped behind it in case this was a robber. She snatched up her notebook and held it in front of her, prepared to use it as a club if necessary.

To her relief, Clarke's face appeared in her doorway.

"Hey." He looked at her with a distracted appearance. "It's me. I forgot my tickets and didn't want to chance the app on the phone. What are you still doing here?"

He was impeccably turned out in a mint green silk shirt with a dark brown blazer on. The color of the cloth brought out his eyes. His hair had been combed back off his forehead and hung to his shoulders in slight waves. The clothes appeared expensive, moving over his body and showing his well-built form to advantage.

Gesturing to the pile of papers on her desk, Terri picked the top sheet up. "I wanted to balance the accounts before going home." Her voice held a note of apology. "I needed to make sure there would be a label on Monday."

He raised an eyebrow, his eyes turning to her computer screen and then back to her with a question lurking in them. "Of course you did. And?"

"There will be." She ignored the part of her that

would be relieved if the decision went the other way. If they closed, she would have no excuse not to try something else.

Then she remembered another woman held his attention tonight. *Supermodel. Right.* "Where's your date?"

Clarke pointed to the street below. "In the car. She's bored."

Bored? She could think of a lot of things she'd be in a similar situation, and that emotion was very low on the list. Nervous. Excited. Scared. Turned on.

An image of the gorgeous model floated into her mind, courtesy of the internet and Ariana's social media. From the gushing tone of the page she had found, Terri guessed the site was run by a fan. "When you're as stunning as Ariana, you expect to be entertained."

Turning away, she began arranging the papers on her desk.

She heard a sigh, and then he was behind her. He was so close she could feel his breath against her neck. Clarke rested his palms on her shoulders, turning her until she could see out the large plate glass windows in the twelfth-story office.

"Take in your surroundings." He pointed toward the window, his exhalation tickling her ear. "Really see them. People are living and enjoying life right now, not stuck at a desk being a one-woman Girl Friday."

The warmth of his hands on her shoulders made her mind a muddle. Her thoughts were further jumbled when he started caressing her in small movements. He was just gliding his fingers back and forth, but her mouth went dry.

"It's got to be done." She was annoyed when the sentence came out husky. "Somebody has to take care of the bottom line."

His breath caught, and he shifted closer. The caresses became longer, still gentle, but now sweeping down to her biceps and back up again.

Her mind was screaming for her to step away, break off this embrace that made her office hot and confining.

"Come with me," he said. "I'll tell Ariana I have to take a work colleague. Believe me, she won't care. We could swing her home, and she'd be fine. She's newly sober and only going out with me because her sponsor told her she should face her fears. She didn't want to keep this date. I'm surprised she did."

In a sudden movement he clasped his hands around her waist and drew her against him. Her butt was nestled against his awakening body. She went to push his hands away and then stopped as a savage flood of desire swept over her. Instead she rested her hands on top of his, across his knuckles.

"Clarke." She turned to meet the fierce green of his eyes.

"Shh, shh, I know you won't say yes, trust me. Life is going on around you, babe, while you waste your days stuck in this office." His hands were clamped tight, holding her against his hardening body. "You need to make fun a priority, Miss August. Every time I get here, you're here, and every time I leave, you're here. Life is too short to spend your time propping up a failing record label. You deserve more than that." He turned his head until he could kiss her in a feather-light caress. His tongue dipped inside when her short exhalation of breath opened her mouth to his.

She wanted to protest, but all she managed was a throaty murmur that sounded like assent.

"Terri," he whispered, brushing her hair back from her face.

She moved to push him away, but instead her hands went to his hips, encouraging his body when he rocked against hers. She had gone too long without feeling the warmth of male skin under her fingers. She couldn't remember the last time she had touched the sculpted muscles of a man's hard chest and the different, exciting planes of the masculine body.

She would be able to tell herself that if she'd ever reacted to a man the way she responded to him. She'd never wanted to slip her hands under cloth so she could feel a masculine heartbeat. It had been years since she had the desire to throw her body around his, crawl on top of him, and let him thrust inside her until they were one and could never be separated.

She didn't resist when he slid his callused palms over her bare skin and found her bra. She cursed the fact that she'd put on the seamless white cotton one today, wishing she had on some fragile lace concoction instead. His teeth bit the nape of her neck before he started raining kisses along her hairline at the same time he unbuttoned the blouse. Finally, the cloth lay open, draping across her torso, neither concealing nor revealing.

Terri shuddered, throwing her head back to meet the warm muscle of his chest. A throaty growl of satisfaction emitted from him at her involuntary movement, and he slid her free of the cups and molded her breasts with his hands.

"Clarke." Her voice was breathy, the silent plea obvious. Catching her nipple between thumb and forefinger, he tugged on the small nub.

White lightning streaked through her, and she sagged. One of his arms went around her, holding her body against his while the other continued to play with her. Finding her lips again, he thrust his tongue into her mouth while his free hand caressed first one then the other breast. She began to whimper, sounds he caught with his mouth and took into his throat.

He kissed her a few minutes longer before he drew back and released her, his eyes a vivid green that leaped off his face. He gripped her shoulders to steady her and then put her clothes back in place until no mark of his touch was visible.

Her mind reeled, her body still shaking in the aftermath. "I… You…"

Bemusement lurked behind the intense need in his eyes. "Damn, you're a good kisser. There's a passionate woman behind that business exterior."

"I can't believe I just kissed you." She'd often dreamed of throwing down on the conference table, but she never had anyone she wanted to ask.

He cupped her cheek in his palm and forced her to meet his gaze. "*We* just kissed, Tyris August. Not just you, not just me. Both of us. I loved it. I want more."

"But all we did was kiss…well…" She half expected him to unzip his fly and push her head down to his groin. The idea of sliding his member into her mouth thrilled her, but she had no idea how to initiate that sort of conversation.

"Kissing is a start. Walk out with me."

Nodding her head in silent acquiescence, she shut

down her computer and then gathered her things.

They walked through the office and down the semi-dark corridor toward the elevator in silence. Before they reached the door, he took her shoulders and swung her against the wall.

"Come with me, please. I don't want to be with the Arctic supermodel. I want to spend the night with you." He kissed her again, their noses bumping before he aligned their heads to meld their lips together. Terri suspected if she accepted his invitation, they would end the evening in his bed. He pressed against her pelvic bone, tempting her with the promise of his erection. She had to go now, or there was no turning back.

"I can't think straight. You have a date. You should go."

A muscle jumped in the back of his jaw, but he stepped back from her and nodded. "You first. I need a minute to, uh, get myself back together."

She took in the bulge in the front of his pants before she looked up at him. His face was twisted with raw hunger that showed in his clenched teeth and taut body.

"See you Monday." She ducked into the elevator when it dinged. Clarke didn't follow.

****

A bell kept going off as she flew around the skyscraper. The persistent buzz interrupted her enjoyment of the open sky and gleaming windows. It kept on and on until finally she grumbled and surfaced out of sleep. The factory-installed ringtone of her cell phone had never been so annoying. Terri glanced at the clock, which read a little after midnight. She knew who the person had to be even before the Caller ID on her phone confirmed his identity.

"Clarke," she said, her voice groggy with sleep. "How was the show?"

His voice was gravelly. "Good. We haven't got a snowball's chance in hell of signing them. I gave them my card and suggested meeting, but they didn't bite. Lorenzo Thomas from Earthy Cry Records was lurking, and their manager was talking to him. The meeting was very friendly. One of the band members wanted my autograph, but that was all they were interested in."

Her stomach twisted. Apposite was becoming the label of last resort, but the awareness still stung. "I worked for Lorenzo before I went to work for Kai. He gets what he wants. Did you give the guy your signature?"

"Of course. I took pictures with fans, and it's already been reposted dozens of times. I'm good for something."

She shouldn't say the next words but did so anyway. "How did the supermodel like the show?"

His chuckle zinged through the phone lines like a balm to her senses. "She spotted Will Bevison from my old label and beelined for him. He was only interested in the band. I tried to find her before I left, but she wasn't around. I hope she's still sober. That's not up to me, though. You could have come with me. She would have been grateful."

"Clarke…" Relief flooded her at his lack of attraction to the gorgeous, perfect model.

"Her looks are her vessel, not who she is. But that's not why I called."

Holding the phone in one hand, Terri fumbled for her nightstand light and then slapped at her pillows until she was propped up against her headboard.

"Why did you call, then? Not that I mind, but you don't usually phone." She didn't say what was echoing in her mind, that she was grateful for the confirmation that he wasn't interested in Ariana. It would make her weekend much easier. Was he still wearing that gorgeous green shirt he'd had on at the beginning of the night? Or was he dressed in something else? Nothing else?

"I wanted to apologize. I kissed you without permission, I mauled your breasts, and I craved doing a whole lot besides that. I acted on impulse and didn't think about your feelings."

She coughed, disappointment burrowing into her soul. She was glad he wasn't there to witness the pain she would have been unable to hide. The reason he was calling was to make amends. Life sucked.

Her next words were low and flat as she struggled to keep the hurt out of them. "Are you sorry you kissed me?"

His intake of breath shot through her muddled brain. "Hell no. I loved feeling you writhe in my arms. If I could repeat the experience, I wouldn't change a thing. Except ask first. It's not good to take."

"Oh." She gripped the phone so tightly that the case made a cracking sound. "I'm not upset."

"Good."

"Is that the only reason you called? To apologize?" She wasn't aware she was going to pose the question until the words came out of her mouth.

A pause on the other end, a silence so deep she wasn't sure he was going to answer.

"You're not mad? About me kissing you?"

"Not at all. Thank you for your apology, but I'm not sorry you did."

He let out a long sigh. "Thanks. I am still learning about women, even at my age." He said the words with a distinct edge in his tone.

A thousand ways to respond danced in her mind, but all of them stuck in her throat. "I know how you feel." The words were inadequate. If she had courage, she could initiate a different conversation, but she couldn't get the sentences out.

"Huh."

She waited for him to say something else, but all that came through the line was his breathing. "Clarke? Are you still there?"

"I'm here," he replied and let out a breath. "I don't know you very well. I want to, though. What I think I understand keeps getting turned on its head."

"Clarke, I'm…"

"Don't apologize. Please. It takes time to build trust. I am still learning that instant intimacy isn't the healthiest way to begin a relationship."

"Is that—" She couldn't finish. She couldn't. Then she summoned her courage and soldiered on despite the butterflies slamming around in her gut. "—what we're doing?" She burrowed into the covers, throwing her comforter over her body and burying her face in its soft warmth.

"I can't say what we're doing, babe." His reply was followed by a short silence. "It feels like we've taken it beyond friends, but it's too soon to put a label on it. That okay with you?"

She didn't know this man. The Clarke she knew ten years ago was not the man of today. No, she didn't know him. But she wanted to. "It's okay. More than okay."

"Thanks." He took a deep breath. "This is new territory for me, Terri. Bear with me?"

"If you will with me." She plucked the thick brown and white comforter away from her and stared at the window. She was breathing so rapidly that she put a hand to her chest to calm her body. The outside world was quieter at this time of night, except for a television blaring in the apartment building next door. A car horn sounded on the heavily traveled street just a half a block away. Even at this hour, the city wasn't at rest.

"Yeah. That's what I want." His words were raspy yet smooth in a seductive blend of emotion. "The supermodel had nothing on you."

"Clarke…" His name was the only word she was capable of.

"I couldn't let you end your night thinking I wanted to be with her, not after the way I kissed you. I am aware of my rep, babe, but that's not me these days."

Memories flooded her, of a time at the Whammy Bar when she had managed to get his attention, only to be told to leave when the latest hot model walked in. It had devastated her then, and the memory still stung. Tears pricked her eyes at the long-ago pain, and she had to force herself to speak. "Thank you. It does…matter."

"Good." He clipped off the word. For a moment she thought he was going to say something else, but he remained silent.

He was an almost tangible presence in her bedroom. The remembered feel of his lips filled her with renewed sensation. She had so much she wanted to say but lacked the words—and the courage.

She yawned, her jaw cracking with the motion. "It's late, and I've got work tomorrow. We've got work tomorrow," she amended hastily. "I hate to end this, but I'm starting to feel the hour." Her eyelids were growing heavy, despite the tingle in her body.

"Got it. My bad. Will you stay on the phone a little longer? I'd love to drift off together. It would be like I was there."

"Yeah. I will. Good night, Clarke."

"Good night, gorgeous Terri. Sweet dreams. Hope I'm in them."

"I was dreaming of flying, but I suspect that might change." Despite herself, she was beginning to fade. "It would be nice to think I was in yours as well." Uncertainty pierced her even as she said the words. The entire conversation was as close as she had gotten to being vulnerable with him—or any man—in the last ten years. He might not understand what it cost her to ask, but she did.

"You already are. Terri?"

"Yes?" Her voice was muffled, weariness beginning to claim her. She wanted to stay on the phone and not let this magic moment end, but her body wasn't letting her.

"Have dinner with me tomorrow night?"

"I'd like that."

His voice was gentle. "Great. So would I. If I were there, I'd tell you to put your head on my shoulder and say good night. Do that. I'll sing you a lullaby as you drift off, Terri August."

She curled around her pillow, wishing it were Clarke. He was crooning Brahms' "Lullaby" as she adjusted her covers until she was comfortable. She laid the phone down where she could still hear him, the screen bright against her sheets.

Within minutes, she was asleep.

Chapter Seven

"What are you hungry for?" Terri hoped her voice didn't betray her quaking insides.

"Not the Whammy Bar," Clarke said, naming the place where he used to hang out.

She shuddered. "Oh God, no."

The rock holdover might have outlived its heyday but was still a place where fading stars had their moments of former glory. She doubted they still had her banned from the place, but couldn't take that chance. It would be far too easy for someone to remember the past and expose her for the fraud she was.

"How about Gladstone's in Malibu? We can get crab and lobster and then go down to the beach for a walk." He turned his attention back to the road but not before meeting her gaze for a searing moment. The passion in his eyes showed a banked desire that heated her blood.

"Sounds good."

His luxury car was an older model but still gleamed like new. It cut the road cleanly in the late afternoon twilight. The sun was setting in the west, bright and hot, beaming down onto the street and filling the car with light. He put on a pair of sunglasses, blocking her view of his eyes.

They made small talk as they drove toward the Pacific Coast Highway. In a strange way she had known him forever. He fit like a piece of clothing she took out of her closet when she needed something comfortable to wear. She had never in a million years believed she would say that about Clarke Masters.

You stalked him, she reminded herself. *He sent you a letter and threatened you with a restraining order. You've got no business being around him.*

Shut up, she told her inner critic.

"I haven't been here in years," she said as they pulled onto the freeway that ran along the Pacific Ocean.

"You work too hard, babe." He stroked her hand before returning his to the stick shift.

"True." She slid her hand over his hair-roughened one and squeezed. "It feels good to relax."

The grin he flashed her stripped years from his face. "Glad to hear it. I worry about you. You take things so hard."

"I need to," she retorted.

"I know. Not tonight, though."

They were in the parking lot before she could respond. A valet handed her out of the car. Clarke tucked her hand into his.

"No thinking," he whispered as he put her hand against his waist and slung his arm around her shoulder. "This is fantasy. Don't spoil the mood."

She shivered and ran her nails over his waist.

He sucked in his breath. "Terri, don't tease."

She halted, and he moved before stopping when she failed to come with him. He must have taken in the stricken expression on her face because he trapped her arm against him when she would have tugged free of his embrace.

"Terri, what?"

"I'm not teasing," she managed. "I'm just out of practice."

He took her hands, playing his thumbs over the sensitive skin of her thumb and forefinger. "I get it." His puzzled tone said he didn't.

She should tell him, but she couldn't bear to watch the light in his eyes fade as he recognized what a lunatic she'd been ten years earlier. Better to let the secret burn within her than lose what was happening between them.

The waves crashing over the rocks on the beach drew her attention. Between the valet parking area and Gladstone's, a path led down to the rocks. Seagulls soared over the vista, and in the distance the horn of a very large ship sounded as it made its way across the water.

"Can we go down there after dinner?" She gestured to the water.

"I promised, didn't I? I keep my promises." He threaded his fingers through hers and raised her hand to his lips for a kiss. "No thinking, babe, not tonight. Just let it happen. Let's enjoy each other."

"Not thinking is tough for me, but I'll try."

"That's all I can ask." He kissed her hand again and restored her arm to around his waist.

****

The fresh-faced young kid seating people showed no recognition when Clarke gave his name and time of reservation. His polite smile held that of a server doing his job. Within minutes they were seated across from each other at a table with wooden benches for seats.

She searched for some sort of recognition from

other people, but nobody turned in their direction. She remembered times back in the day when Clarke couldn't walk into the Whammy Bar without causing a sensation. She'd thought she liked the adulation that went with his fame, but now she wondered.

"Does it bother you when people don't recognize you?"

He had gloried in it as well, judging by the interviews he gave. Fame was a drug, he'd said, along with all the other good stuff he had available. Now it, like him, was faded.

"Some do, trust me. A couple of online sites are set up specifically to cater to Big Bad Clarke Masters. I had to stop letting people see when I was online, because it got overwhelming. I'm old news, but not gone." His gaze took in the restaurant.

His face twisted a little, and then he focused his attention on her. "Does it bug me that I don't get the cars and the women and the attention thrown at me? Does it bother me that I don't have people dogging my every move and trying to take pictures through my windows? Back then I could lift a finger and get anything I wanted. Women, wine, drugs, whatever I craved. I didn't have to do anything for myself, and I liked it that way. Does it upset me that I don't run with a posse whose sole goal in life is to get me what I need and enable any rotten behavior I have?"

He leaned over so only she could hear him. "No. I was a monster back then. How I treated women— everyone—was appalling, and I regret it. My band hates me, and so do most of the people I interacted with at that time. Women…there were so many. Hundreds, thousands probably. My memory is fuzzy on that score." He shot her a glance, his face shifting into chagrin. "That's in the past. I mean, I haven't been doing that lately," he amended. "Since I've been clean, things are different. I don't get how to date these days." He made a self-deprecating gesture. "Those I hurt would say I'm getting what I deserve."

This would be the perfect time to confess their past relationship. She could remind him about his "little Maine stalker" and reassure him the woman she was today wasn't that person. Instead, she touched the back of his hand, sliding her palm along his skin. He turned his hand over with a swift move and laced their fingers together. Yes, now was the perfect time.

She couldn't do it. It would change everything, and while she intellectually knew she needed to do it, she couldn't bear the aftermath. He had to remember the pesky Lynx, the woman who would not leave him alone. It would alter everything he understood about her, and Terri wasn't ready for that. It might be chicken of her, but she wasn't. She would have to—she was aware of that. Later. Not yet.

His wounded gaze searched hers, despair written on his face. "You won't hold my past against me, will you? That's all that is. I can't change it, but I can make today better. I don't have what I once did. I'm not much of a catch, but I think I'm a better guy today than I was. If you're willing, I'd like to take this to the next level."

What she held against him was very different than he imagined, but the answer was no in both cases. "I won't hold it against you." *If you'll do the same for me.* "Once I did, yes, but I've been around you enough to understand you've changed."

Shadows tugged his lips down in grief. "Hope so. I

hope you give this a chance. One day at a time."

Even though it was wrong not to be honest with him, she stayed quiet. She hated to think about ten years ago. She didn't want to lose the admiration in his eyes. Terri hoped he took the flush on her cheeks for desire, not shame.

"One day at a time. That's all anyone can do." One day at a time, for her as well. For the first time in ages, a man desired her—needed her. Even if the feeling was temporary, it was lovely.

He flexed his fingers against hers, the warmth of his skin sending electricity skidding through her.

****

Low tide stretched the sand far beyond the boulders when they made their way down to the Malibu shoreline. Water glittered in the distance. Shells and rocks dotted the landscape along with cigarette butts, discarded cups, and other litter.

They picked their way to the sandy area, and then he came to a halt, leaning against a large rock. Since dinner he had not stopped touching her, gripping her hands, gliding over her hair, pressing his knees against hers under the table. The attention made her feel like a giddy teenager.

"Come here," he said, yanking her against him. "I've been dying to kiss you all night. Now I have to in this place where there's nothing but sand, salt, and you and me."

The gleam of moonbeams reflected in his eyes. Primitive, feral need lurked behind his smile, like a leopard stalking his prey. Slipping her arms around him, she kneaded his shoulders as she tilted her head up to his. The smell of salt and seaweed competed with his musky cologne before his scent overwhelmed her.

No other beachgoers were nearby on this stretch of sand. The faint sounds of the restaurant were audible above them and the splash of the waves behind.

He flashed a quick grin, and then his lips were on hers, sliding over her gently and nuzzling her with soft kisses.

When she licked him with her tongue, he made a thick sound and gathered her close, his hands wrapping around her waist until they were pressed together.

Clarke widened his stance. Bracing their bodies against the rock, he brought her into full contact with his body.

"If our positions were reversed, I would say I'd be caught between a rock and a hard place," she joked, sliding her groin over his.

"I'm caught between a rock and a soft place," he murmured, grazing his teeth over her earlobe. She shivered as his breath swirled in her ear. "No place I'd rather be." Delving his tongue into her, he licked again and then bit her lobe.

Terri jerked, and her breathing quickened. "Kiss me," she begged. "Really kiss me."

His hand was still at the nape of her neck, and he clasped her hair, moving her head back for his touch. She let it fall, wanting only to feel his lips. When he touched her again, she whimpered.

He thrust into her mouth with an intense claiming. He tasted the edges of her teeth, and then tangled his tongue with hers, spearing her again and again until she was clutching at him, her nails digging into the shoulders of his jacket. She was pressed against him, their bodies meeting in a smooth line. Heat poured off his body as he began moving against her, beating out the same rhythm of need and desire.

"I want you." He ground the words out while he separated her legs with his thigh before thrusting closer.

Looking around to make sure nobody was close enough to see what she was doing, she placed a hand on his straining erection and squeezed. He jumped and then thrust into her hand.

"That much?" she asked in wonder.

"More."

She removed her hand and slid both hands up the lapels of his jacket until she linked them at the back of his neck.

"Then, yes. Definitely yes. Can you walk?" She kissed his jaw and his Adam's apple with light nips of her tongue, and once again he shuddered.

"Not...sure. I won't be able to if you keep that up." With his forehead pressed against hers, Clarke didn't say anything for long moments, his breathing rapid. "I think I can manage," he said, meeting her gaze. "Are you sure you want this?"

She tried to push the memory of their last time out of her mind. This time would be different. They were older, wiser, and not the same people they were before. "I want you. I'm afraid..." She let the words trail off, the memory of that first time and all the subsequent failures sending ripples of fear through her body. *Little Maine stalker,* echoed in her mind. *If you want to play with the big dogs, you have to learn better tricks.* She hadn't learned those behaviors, and she was barely adequate in bed. "I want you."

****

He was going over the speed limit but eased up

when she cast a nervous glance at the speedometer. Years ago he would have screamed around curves, and if he got pulled over, too bad. He drove a stick shift and kept removing his hand from the inside of her thigh to switch gears, but always returned his fingers to the sensitive skin. She caressed him, sliding over the hard flesh, feeling his body tighten as she touched him. Moonlight poured through the windows, competing with the harsh glow of street lights and neon signs.

"Townhouse." He drove down Sunset Boulevard as fast as he could. Traffic caught up to them, and he ground his teeth, showing his frustration at the slow speed.

"Townhouse," he repeated. "I'd never survive the trip to Glendale."

He slid his hand over her thigh and under the skirt of her dress until he was resting above her heat.

"Oh God," he groaned when his fingers encountered her slick readiness. Then he withdrew his hand, tucking the cloth back around her legs.

"I don't want to get stopped for public indecency." Taking the opportunity of yet another stoplight, he delved his tongue into her mouth with a quick, hard stroke.

Finally, they were at his place. When they swung into his parking space, Clarke threw the brake on and grabbed for her hand. He pushed her into the elevator with almost indecent haste and jammed his finger at his floor button until the light went on.

His eagerness was bringing back memories of that rushed, unpleasant time. Apprehension darted over her skin. She opened her mouth to speak, but he was kissing her, his fingers hard on her shoulders as he pushed her to the back wall, and she blazed hot in her response.

"Clarke," she whispered when he released her. His eyes were heated fire, burning her as they moved over her body.

The bell dinged and the door opened, and he thrust his hand in hers and tugged her forward. The place was dark, but he guided her to the dimly lit bedroom at the far end of the foyer. He swung her inside and closed the door. He carried her to the bed and came down on top of her with a heavy thud.

She pushed against the cloth that threatened to smother her. He eased up, bracing on his arms before bending to kiss her. She took a sharp breath, feeling the edges of his teeth with her tongue as her hands stole around his neck.

He stripped off his jacket, dumping it on the floor. The heavy rise and fall of his chest drew her attention, his heart beating visibly against the cloth. She should have been reassured at his obvious readiness, but dread curled inside her. He unbuttoned his shirt and also threw that aside. His muscled, furred chest was glorious and scary.

"Get naked. Now."

He moved and zipped down his pants, kicking off his shoes at the same time. Savage need suffused his face. He didn't appear to have much control.

Or maybe he didn't want to slow things down. Like last time. *Little Maine stalker.* Still she did as he wanted, sliding the top over her head until her torso was bared. After removing her bra, she let both articles fall before she bent to unzip her bottom. She removed the skirt and thong off her legs and turned her attention back to him.

He was hard and ready, and he was amazing. Things were going to be fine.

"Dear God." He covered her with his body again. "You are way off the charts."

Holding her hair, he kissed her again with fierce intensity. Terri began to feel an answering echo of desire in her body. He slid a hand down her and raked his nails over her nipples, which leaped to life.

Things would be all right.

He shuddered again and moved to the nightstand. "I have to be inside you now. Now."

She wasn't ready. She was getting there, but she hadn't warmed up yet. Still she nodded her acceptance, not knowing what else to do. He donned a condom and faced her with an expectant stare.

Then he was over her, and in one motion Clarke entered her, filling her.

Ten years and several lovers hadn't changed anything. She still couldn't please a man. He wanted to get it over with, just like last time. She accepted his claiming, lying back with a defeated sigh.

****

A dim corner of his mind told him she had stopped responding. Need knocked him flat, and he shuddered, thrusting all the way inside her. He wanted to wait and slow down, but his primal brain took over, his passion burning through everything else. He had lost control, but any rational thought was wiped out by the orgasm that pounded through him. A cry tore from his throat. Clenching her shoulders, he thrashed against her, pouring inside as the maelstrom of his climax took him. It went on and on, the pleasure savaging him with its intensity. He couldn't stop. He couldn't do more than ride out the wave that took him to new heights. It would have been the most glorious moment of his life, if she were there with him.

When it finally ended, he sighed and pressed his face against hers. She was hot to the touch but was lying still. He moved next to her, careful not to collapse and crush her with his weight, and took her in his arms, holding her. He waited, wondering what she was going to do. Terri said nothing, her arms lying at her sides even as her body was pressed against his. She was staring at the far wall as though she were in another country and not lying tangled in his sheets.

Clarke reviewed the last rollercoaster moments and groaned inwardly. He'd plunged into her like a savage, ripping through her defenses and taking her before she was ready. He'd been nearly blind with desire, but that was not a reason. Need was no excuse. Desire was no excuse. He studied her face again, but only emptiness lay there when she met his gaze. The truth was evident in the desolation behind those gray eyes. Still she said nothing, her attention somewhere behind him.

He couldn't doubt the truth. The sex had been a disaster. Never in his life had he lost control like this. He hadn't allowed her time to warm up or done anything to help the process once they got to his place. Hell, he'd barely given her time to get her clothes off. He suspected that she removed them fearing he would tear them off her if she didn't deal with them. Her excitement in the car had been just that, excitement, and he hadn't built on it. He'd behaved as he once had, with no concern for his partner, only for his needs. He was supposed to have outgrown that failing.

He rolled to his side, separating from her and staring at the far wall. He had no idea what he was supposed to do now. Behind him, Terri shifted, the bed moving under her weight.

"You probably want to go." He tried not to put any emotion into his voice. Who wouldn't want to clear out and away from him, after that performance? She deserved someone who was going to caress every inch of her and make her feel cherished and special. Instead she'd gotten a man with the manners of a caveman. Worse, because he was supposed to be civilized. He ran his hand over his eyes and through his hair, loathing himself. He had no idea how he was going to make amends for this. She wouldn't—shouldn't—forgive him.

He imagined he heard a sob. She climbed from the bed, validating his belief. From the creaking of the floorboards, he understood she was gathering her scattered belongings. He wanted to turn to her, beg her forgiveness, and make this right, but he doubted his touch would be welcome. Not after that fiasco. The best thing he could do would be to let her leave his townhouse and forget this disaster ever happened.

Despite his desire to go to her, he stayed turned away from her, his body rigid, hands fisting against his chest. He had to let this happen. He had been inconsiderate, and the least he could do was let her make a retreat gracefully.

Although every instinct was screaming for him to explain, he stayed quiet. He had to let her go. It was the right thing to do.

Chapter Eight

Terri found her clothes and began dressing as fast as she could, wanting to get out of the townhouse and away from her humiliating failure. Her fingers trembled so hard she couldn't manage her bra for several moments until she wrested the hooks over her aching breasts. Her shirt was wrong side out, and she had a few bad moments before managing to straighten it and get it on. She yanked the skirt back on with trembling hands, dashing her hands at the visible wrinkles where he had pulled at the cloth in a fury of desire.

She was a failure as a lover. Why hadn't she learned that? This man had been the first person to teach her that fact, and he might be the last. She didn't have what it took.

The rest of her clothes were too much. Stuffing her panties into her purse and carrying her shoes in one hand, she took one agonizing look at the stiff lines of his back before retreating to the door. He appeared angry, forbidding. He could have only one reason for his mood. She had promised him so much and let him down in every way he could be let down. Once he was aware how god-awful she was in the sack, he wanted the sex done with. Just like before.

When she was at the door with her hand on the knob, Terri turned around. She watched the quick rise and fall of his body against the mattress for a tense moment before she spoke.

"I'm sorry," she said to his taut back, trying to keep the sobs threatening to build from her voice.

He jerked at that, shifting to face her. She turned away before he could make out the tears lurking on her cheeks.

"I'm sorry," she said again. "I suck at tricks to please a man, and I hate that you felt like you had to get it over with. It won't happen again."

An explosion of breath and a muttered "get it over with…" sounded behind her before the creak of his bed told her he'd gotten up.

Out. She had to get out. He was a much nicer man than he had been ten years prior, but that didn't stop the facts. Truth was truth. She sucked as a lover.

She had the door wrenched open and was almost out of his townhouse when his strong forearm shoved the entrance closed with a bang. Standing unmoving, her hand still on the doorknob, she went rigid with his naked body warm behind her. The tang of cologne and sweat filled her senses, and then he was pressing his body full-length against hers, his arms above her head. The only contact between them was the breadth of his chest and his strong thighs alongside.

"Is that what you think?" he whispered, resting his cheek on the back of her head. "That I wanted to get it over with?"

His husky voice was silk against her ear. Feeling moisture spike her lashes and run down her cheeks, Terri contented herself with nodding. A few strands of his hair fell over her forehead as he stood there, pressed against her, motionless except for the heavy rise and fall of his chest.

"Oh, babe." He brushed her hair back to press a kiss against her cheekbone. His arms went around her waist, drawing her into him. She didn't resist but didn't turn around either, tears still streaking down her face. She closed her hands over his, and he twined their fingers together.

"I didn't want to get it over with." The low, deep tone of his voice was making her shiver again, the want that hadn't been slaked snaking its way through her body. "I intended to linger over you for hours. But, Terri, babe…" He slid to a halt. Turning her around, he groaned out loud at the pained look on her face. She tried to squirm away, but he took a hand and wrapped it around her chin, forcing her gaze back to his. "I got inside you, and I lost control. I tried to stop, but I couldn't. I didn't give you time to warm up or do anything before I was taking you. I'm sorry."

She tried to speak, but she was trembling so hard she couldn't. Tears dropped on her cheeks, but she made no move to wipe them away. Clarke's eyes darkened, and his lips pressed together.

"You believe me, don't you?" he asked. "It's the truth, I swear. This is my failure, not yours." His thumbs wiped away old tears as new ones fell.

She nodded again and met his gaze. Reaching up, she placed her hands on his forearms, the short hairs tickling her palms.

He kissed her eyelashes in a feather caress. "I'll tell you what I wanted to do," he murmured. "Better yet, I'd like to show you."

"But, Clarke, I…I'm no good at sex." She forced the whispered words out, the confession curling inside her belly.

"You know." He stroked her hair. "You're only as good as your partner. I wasn't much of one just now. I took and didn't think of you. I'd like to make up for that. Terri, let me."

She bit her lip. If she failed him again, that would be the end.

"I feel horrible for taking you like I did. Please."

Uncertainly she peered at him again. He pressed a kiss on her forehead and then kissed her hairline. Stroking her back, he held her, and she began to relax in his arms.

"That's good." His lips rested against her ear. Then he turned his head and licked the upper curve of her earlobe with his tongue. She shivered at the light caress. Delving in again, he filled the hollow. Then he moved to the other side and treated her other lobe to the same seduction.

He licked the dip behind her ear and above her jawbone with a swift dart. Again he didn't play favorites. He ran his thumbs down the backs of her ears as he kissed first one and then the other.

Terri slid her hands up his body, across the thick pelt of chest hair, feeling the hard muscles and the still-drying sweat of passion on his skin. She rested them on his shoulders as he bent his head to her. Pressing kisses along her jawline, he tasted the indentation of her chin.

She moved her head down to the heat of his mouth. Clarke turned his head, and their lips met in a brief caress.

His heartbeat accelerated under her palms. He traced the bow of her lips before exploring inside. Meeting his tongue, she pressed even closer to him. He gathered her close, his arms hard at her waist as he continued to kiss her.

Desire pulsed through her again, returning with a suddenness that startled her. "Clarke." She sagged against him. "I don't think I can stand up."

He grinned and then lowered her to the bed.

"Good." He drew back to meet her gaze. The blaze of the lamp illuminated the lower half of his face and cast shadows across his body. "You are overdressed." He skimmed his hands over her curves. "May I?" He lingered at the hem of her shirt as he continued to study her.

"Yes," she said on a breathy moan. His hands were moving, and her brain cells scattered at the feel of his callused palms over the skin of her waist. The cool night air hit her in a rush, but he was there, warming her as he pushed the top farther up to her shoulders. She lifted her arms, and he pulled the blouse over her head and threw it on the floor. Her bra followed the blouse.

"Beautiful," he breathed. "I barely touched them before, and I've wanted to so much. May I?" he asked again, his avid gaze fixed on her breasts.

She was incapable of anything except nodding. He continued his slow exploration of her head and neck, kissing the column and her collarbone. He bit her shoulder and nuzzled her armpit. Terri jumped at the unexpected mixture of ticklish and earthy sensuality.

"Clarke," she whispered.

He licked her again and a spiral of sensation lashed her body.

"Feels good, doesn't it." He moved down her side and nipped at her skin with light bites.

"Yes." She shuddered under the sensual nips, pleasure mingling with the jolt every time he touched her.

"Told you I wanted to cover you in love marks," he said before switching his attention to the other side and repeating his actions. "Do you mind?"

The part of her that was still rational wondered if she was going to have to wear long sleeves for a few days, but the rest of her didn't care.

"No. I don't mind."

He covered her breasts with his big hands. "Except these. I don't want to mark these gorgeous things in any way." He bent down and drew her nipple into his mouth without preamble, his hands kneading them as he sucked. Her hands laced through his mane of blond hair, holding him against her body as she writhed under him.

"Oh yeah, that's it," he said against her body. "That's what I want to feel. You, under me, moving against my body." His member began hardening against her hip. Terri gloried in the sensation.

Clarke suckled both breasts until they were taut, and then raised his head to examine his handiwork. A mixture of need and desire washed through her. Clarke outlined the ruby-tipped puckered nipples, and this time she cried out, thrusting in wild abandon. Her mouth opened and closed on her gasps of breath, and her hips undulated.

He scanned her body, and she knew he could see the flush on her skin and the sweat misting her. "I was going to take this slow, lick and bite you, but I don't think you want to wait. What do you think, Terri? Do you want to come?"

She should have been embarrassed, but his words were dampening her further. "Yes," she said, scoring his back with her nails and pressing her fingers into his shoulders.

He slid his hand down between her legs. "Good. I want to make you come too." Moving, he showed her that he was erect again. "How do you want it?"

She squirmed, an action that had nothing to do with arousal. "I…"

"There is no right or wrong answer. Your pleasure." As he spoke he moved his hand, delving into her ready heat and caressing her nub with his thumb.

"I want it all." She arched against him. "But…but your tongue first? I've never had good oral sex, and I've always wanted to know…" She broke off.

"My pleasure. Look at me."

Her gaze met his again. Without breaking eye contact, he went down her body, kissing the skin he encountered along the way. With deft movements he slid the skirt off her waist, and she kicked the cloth to the floor. She assumed he would break off when he reached the juncture between her legs, but he didn't. Instead, with his gaze still on hers, he extended his tongue and traced her lower lips.

"Oh, Terri, you're so ready. Just for me."

She started to close her eyes, but a sharp movement stopped her.

"Keep them open," he ordered. "Watch me taste you."

He parted her farther. She lost all sense of time and went limp. Desire cascaded through her, spiraling her tighter and higher. Before she could climax, Clarke backed off, substituting his fingers and exploring inside her. Then he covered her nub with his teeth and gripped her in his mouth.

Her head lolled back. Terri surrendered to the sensation of his body until everything came down to the agony of need in the pit of her stomach. The pressure of his teeth and the incessant caress of his mouth pushed her over the edge. Crying out, she arched against him a final time, her climax swamping her with its force. She was flung into ecstasy, shuddering and shaking as the sensations pounded on and on through her.

"Clarke!" Her cry was an exultation as she let go of her moorings and spun into an unfamiliar universe. The climax went on for an eternity, shaping the world into new dimensions.

When she regained her senses, he was still buried between her legs, his head resting to one side. His breathing was hot against her open flesh.

"You taste so good, baby." To her astonishment, his lips were on her. Within seconds she was crying out again, the orgasm that hadn't quite finished rippling through her on a renewed wave. Terri clutched at his shoulders as a second pinnacle tore through her. For a moment she was afraid she would leave the earth and never return.

"Yeah." He raised his head and met her gaze. "That's more like it." He rolled off her and removed a condom from the nightstand. "I want you again, babe. Are you ready for me?"

She took the packet from his hands and ripped the foil open. She stared at the condom while he breathed hard, his erect penis pointing toward her. She met his gaze and then rolled the latex over him until he was sheathed.

He emitted a moan at her touch. "Damn, you feel good." He urged her onto her back and positioned himself over her again. Instead of plunging inside her as before, he took his time, filling her until they were one. His arms were rigid, and his head was thrown back in concentration, eyes closed as he began to pant.

His eyes opened, and he kissed her again. "I'm too far gone to be of much use to you, but can you come again? If you can, touch yourself so we can come together. I'd like that."

"Clarke." She was shocked and excited at the same time by the suggestion.

"Please."

She did as he asked, feeling her body under her hand as she touched herself in the way that took her to her peak. He continued to move with her, throwing back his head on a groan.

"Oh yeah, I feel you. You're so hot, so..." He trailed off and then began moving faster. He ducked his head, and his hair fell over onto her neck as he thrust harder. She gasped, the combination of him inside her and the tension on her body making her cry out.

"Clarke!" She cried out the one word as she came apart again. She dug her free hand into his hip, encouraging his body against hers.

"Terri, love," he shouted and went deep. His pulse beat within her as he gave everything he had to her in a wild rush, dancing inside her.

Several moments later, he relaxed. Rolling to the side, he slid out of her and looped his arms around her.

Love? The word was just sex talk, something a man shouted out in orgasm. Still, that particular word on his lips after all that had happened between them filled her with a sense of peace she hadn't felt in a long time.

"Go to sleep." He stroked her hair with his hand. "I have to regain my strength for tomorrow."

Chapter Nine

The light streaming past thick wooden vertical-blind slats told her it was mid-morning. His side of the bed was cool to the touch, but the indentation on his pillow was still there. He'd tucked the remaining covers around her naked body as she slept.

She found and turned on the bedside lamp and let her eyes adjust to the filtered light. Her clothes were scattered over the floor, evidence of his haste to remove them the night before. She grinned, searing memories of his touch heating her blood again.

A strange odor was in the air, mixing with his lingering cologne and the earthy sweats of their shared passion. She reached down and grabbed his shirt lying in a heap on the floor. Terri slipped it over her bare torso after shaking out the worst of the wrinkles. The bedroom was still and quiet, hushed in the morning hour.

She padded over to the closed door and peered out of the bedroom, which opened into a long hallway. To the right was the living room and the kitchen, but she had no idea what lay in the other direction. She peeked into the first room and then the kitchen in case Clarke was in there, but they were empty. Her bladder was full, lending urgency to her need to find him.

Turning to the left increased the smell, reminding her of the time she'd painted her childhood bedroom.

Sounds came from the other end of the hall.

She tiptoed to the room and knocked on the door. "Clarke?" she called, and the scratching stopped. The scent was almost overwhelming, leaving no doubt that the stench emanated from this room.

"Yeah, hold on a sec." There was a *whoomp*, like a large cloth being aired out, and then a heavy rustle. "Come on in."

She pushed on the door and blinked, fumes assaulting her eyes. A ceiling fan above made lazy circles but didn't do much to cut the smell. Her eyes widened at the sight in front of her.

Canvases of all shapes and sizes were stacked on top of each other against the walls. Clarke, clad only in a pair of boxers, strode to the other window and cracked the bottom open. The vapors began subsiding. She coughed once before the stink started to dissipate.

He was gorgeous in daylight, the dark blond hair of his chest, legs, and arms glinting with sunlight and catching on the sheen of his skin. His underwear clung to his hips and outlined his penis.

He was stripping off thin plastic gloves as he moved back toward her. Clarke flung them to a wastebasket next to an easel covered with a large drop cloth. He grinned at her, gesturing to her body. "Nice shirt. Looks better on you than me."

She glanced around. "What's this?" she asked, doing a three-sixty turn before facing him again.

Red stained his cheeks. "One of the things they encourage you to do in rehab is to find a hobby to occupy your time. I discovered painting." He repeated her gesture, pivoting around the room with his arms flung out. "As usual, I went a little overboard." He pointed to the front wall. "Those are the first ones I did."

Landscapes and abstracts and portraits were everywhere, piled over each other. The early paintings didn't have a direction and were quick, heavy brushstrokes without much form. The later ones began to form a style, which her untrained eye labeled as surrealist.

"So…" Understanding slowly crept through her as she studied the paintings again. Their mystery artist was in every stroke of the brush. "Your friend, the painter. He's you."

He nodded and ducked his head. "I hope you don't mind."

"That makes compensation easier." Her gaze was drawn to the covered easel, and Terri raised an eyebrow.

He caught her glance and moved to the painting. "This one is a work in progress." He stroked the heavy tarp almost lovingly but made no move to take the covering off. "I'm superstitious, babe. I don't show anyone my stuff until I'm happy with the results."

Even though her dismay was silly, his refusal stung a little. She walked to him, fighting nerves as she did so. "Nature calls." She slid her arms around him and tilted her face up to his. "And I could use a toothbrush and a comb through my hair, if you don't mind. I don't know where the bathroom is."

"I like your hair messy." He speared his fingers through the mass. "I like the idea my hands did that. C'mon." He dropped a light kiss on her mouth. "I'll show you where to freshen up. Want to take a shower?"

****

Much later they wound up at local coffee shop within walking distance of his townhouse. Rock and roll memorabilia used to decorate the walls when she frequented the place ten years ago. At one time a large poster of Attraction was behind the cash register, and she used to ask for a table where she could admire the image. More than once she had gone there hoping Clarke would show up.

To her surprise, the poster was still there. Time had ravaged the paper, and a corner was torn, but it still hung in the same spot. The mingled tinge of cooking food and leftover body odor hung in the air, overlaid with a faint scent of smoking grease.

"Nice picture," she said, stroking his arm. A few patrons appeared to recognize him, but they said nothing, turning back to their meals.

His eyes were haunted. The server gestured for them to be seated, cutting off any further discussion of the poster. They had just sat down, menus open, when the waitress interrupted them.

"Can I get you coffee…oh, hi, Clarke."

Clarke glanced at Terri and then up at the woman. "Hi." His face held no trace of recognition.

The woman didn't acknowledge Terri.

"I'm Terri," she said, extending her hand.

The woman's gaze went to Terri's hand, but she made no move to take the proffered palm. "Yvette."

Clarke pressed his foot against Terri's and left it there. "Hi, Yvette." He gave the waitress a once-over before smiling. "How are things?"

Yvette's lips curled. "Still same old, same old. You want the usual? Coffee and a Denver omelet?"

Terri had it on good authority that he used to

stumble into this place between his forays to the Whammy Bar and back home. She'd trailed after him time and again, disappointed that he hadn't chosen her for the evening.

He nodded, handing the menu back to Yvette, who turned to Terri with a cool glance.

"Um. Coffee. Orange juice and, er, eggs Benedict." She named the first things that caught her eye.

"Sure."

He let out a relieved breath when Yvette retreated. "Thanks for the save, babe."

"Did you come here a lot?" *You know the answer to that.*

He turned sideways in the booth. Studying the posters, he was quiet for a minute.

"Probably much more than I remember." He shuddered and slid his hand over hers. "When I started trying to get sober, I went back to all my old haunts. I found out I'd said and done so many things I don't remember. There was a guy here, I think his name was Dale, and he wanted to fight me. Said I'd been hitting on his girlfriend the month before. I don't remember. Those first years of sobriety, I would slip up, go out, as AA refers to drinking again, go on weekend binges and forget everything I did. I had to go to rehab for help. I was tired of losing time and memory. I'd already lost my friends, my band, and my self-respect. If I didn't change things, I would lose myself. This disease will kill you. It's happened far too often since I've been in the program. One day they're there, and the next they're gone."

She folded her fingers around his. "But you didn't die," she said around the lump in her throat. "You're still alive. You pulled yourself back in time." She put her other hand over their joined hands, the touch warm and alive.

"I tried for two years before I finally got straight." His tone was bitter, tinged with acid. "We made it big when I was in my early twenties, and the lifestyle was impossible to resist. I went in full force and didn't come out until I'd hit bottom. Hell." He squeezed her hand. "You don't want or need to know any of this."

But she did know. Not so much his descent down, but his rise to success and the man he had become after their first number-one hit. After those dark days when he threatened her with legal action, she had tried to block out all things Clarke Masters. Hatred was her way of coping, and she put aside the flashes of wit and intelligence she'd seen in his interviews. Ally told her that Clarke got all his best lines out of a joke book, and that validated her beliefs. She needed to view him as a drug-addled, no-good user without much more to offer than a lost soul with a disease. If he was a loser, then the fact that she was a little Maine stalker was irrelevant. She had been able to cloak herself in self-righteous indignation for a long time.

Now she knew differently. He was tragic, wounded, mortal, and ever so human.

"You're thirty-eight, not three hundred, and the world is still open to you. Paint if that's what you want to do. Do music again if that's your passion. Heck, if you want to learn cooking—" She chuckled when he grimaced. "—I'll teach you that too."

He studied her for a minute, his thumb playing over her hand.

"Sometimes I'd kill for a line." He said it so

matter-of-factly that she started. "I'd die for a drink. I'm still an alcoholic, babe, even if I am clean. I'm a bad bet. I could go out at any time. Don't have too much faith in me."

He tried to jerk his hand away, but she clenched her hands over his.

Yvette arrived with heaped plates of food. She tossed them down and clumped off with a promise to bring fresh coffee.

"Clarke." At the tortured pain in his eyes, her heart contracted. "I'm not the one who needs to believe in you. I can have all the confidence in the world, and my saying so means nothing. If you think you're an addict, then you are. That's for you to decide, not me. If you believe you have the strength, then you win. Only you can say for sure, though. That's not a battle anyone else can fight."

For a moment she thought he was going to get up and leave. His arms flexed against the table, and a wild, fierce hurt was in his eyes. His body was tense, as if he wanted to sweep all the plates on the table onto the ground. Then he collapsed back into the booth, and she breathed a sigh of relief.

"Nobody but me, huh?" He took her hand again and resumed that sweeping motion with his thumb. "And my higher power, according to AA." His expression was bemused rather than angry.

"You know that." The urge to spit out the whole, ugly truth about her rose like bile. She opened her mouth, and the words clogged in her throat before she could get them out.

"I do. But…" He raised his gaze to hers. He was so heartbreakingly magnificent that her breath caught.

"Oh, Clarke, you are amazing," she breathed and then bit her lip at what she had said. The words were something a stalker might say and not what the current Terri had any business uttering.

He grinned. "Thanks. It's between me and my higher power. I've been to plenty of meetings to tell me so. AA says that sometimes the only person between me and a drink is my higher power. But…" He trailed off. "I wouldn't mind a helping hand from a gray-eyed strawberry blonde. She's the only one who I've wanted to be with in so long. AA says, 'Let go, let God,' and that's cool. I have trouble with the whole spiritual thing because I can't bring myself to rely on someone else. My sponsor gets pissed at me, and I try, but I struggle with the idea. If it's okay with you, though…"

An uncertain, restless fear dashed through his face, landing in his eyes.

"If it's okay with you," he continued, "I'd like to ask you to be with me. Not in an AA way, just in a man and woman way. I want you to be part of my life. Hell. I suck at this."

He broke off again and turned in the booth. Their plates of food were getting cold, but that didn't matter. This second chance was a miracle.

"I suck at this too." Instead of touching his hands, she twined her legs around his, linking them at the ankles. She met his gaze without blinking.

"I haven't had a man in my life, not one that stayed. Ever. Nobody wanted to. There was something missing in every relationship I had. So go ahead and beat yourself up all you want for all the failures in your life. If that helps you, have a good time. But remember not all of us were addicts, and lots of us still sucked with the opposite sex."

The warmth of him touched her through the separation between his socks and his jeans. Small points of light danced inside her.

"Oh, Terri. Oh, babe." Coming across the booth, his body still half in his seat, he reached for her and kissed her.

When he released her, his pupils were narrow points and his breathing was shallow.

"Hungry?" he asked, digging into the cooling omelet in front of him. The wink he flashed her way left her no doubt as to the true meaning of his words.

"Starved." She picked up her coffee cup and saluted him with it.

****

Terri toyed with the phone button on her console before pressing the speed dial for Ally. She waited, half hoping and half dreading that her friend would answer. After two rings she heard a soft "hello?"

"Ally, hi, it's me, Terri." Belatedly, she remembered it was Sunday. A day of rest for most, including Ally. Regret burned within her. It had been a mistake to call.

"Hi, Terri." Ally paused, and Terri fancied a million questions rushed through Ally, none of them good. She would make an excuse, hang up, and not tell Ally the reason for her call.

"I…"

"What happened? How was your date?"

She had mentioned the date to Ally over IM but then changed the topic away from any other discussion of it. Her friend, to her surprise, remembered that detail.

She was driving home down Fountain Blvd., that

shortcut between Sunset and Santa Monica Blvds., making her way to her apartment. Her home was her refuge, the place she retreated to in her rare leisure time. Today it seemed different, empty. Not that she would tell Ally that.

"It was almost a disaster, but it turned out all right in the end. We…" She stumbled over her next words. "We wound up sleeping together."

Ally's sucked-in breath left little doubt about her friend's opinion. To Ally's credit she didn't say any of the things that must have been dancing in her mind. "I'm not going to lie. That's a surprise. But maybe it's good. Was it…was it better than before?"

She forgot sometimes that Ally was one of the few people who still remembered her past. She should hang up and let it go. Being vulnerable to people only got her hurt. Nobody would want to be in her life if they understood who she really was. She'd tried that before and gotten burned.

Yet emotion drummed inside her like a heartbeat. She'd done this. She could tell Ally the truth. Forcing herself to speak, Terri continued.

"Clarke was into it." She paused, not saying the words that filled her mind so many times before. *Not the way he wasn't into it before.* "I guess…well, I guess we're kind of dating now." She cursed inwardly. *Too much information, Terri. Ally doesn't want to hear all that.*

"What about you? Were you into it?"

She waited, hoping Ally would fill the void, but there was silence on the other end. "Yeah," she said when it became apparent her friend wouldn't speak. "Yeah."

Ally paused for long moments and then let out another breath. "Good. That's what is important. Terri...listen, just be careful. Clarke hurt you really bad before, and I'd hate for it to happen again."

"That was my fault. You know how I was."

To Terri's surprise, Ally was silent for another string of uncomfortable moments. Maybe Ally hadn't forgotten Clarke's *little Maine stalker* either. They were friends now, but it might still be in her mind.

"You were a twenty-year-old girl infatuated with a rock star. He played you just like he played all the others. He let you trail him around because it stroked his ego. I was there. I remember. Women were disposable to him—to all of them. There's a reason I stopped going out with Harris. You're not the girl you used to be. You're smart, educated, and you have a ton to offer any man bright enough to snap you up. It's your choice this time. Be wise. Don't let him mess with your mind."

The tears that she believed were gone surfaced in her eyes. She pulled into her parking space and sat in the spot, the car idling. There was silence on both ends.

The line beeped, startling Terri out of her funk.

Ally sighed. "Terri, it's Dirk. We have plans. I can cancel them if you want to come over and talk. He's a good guy. He'll understand."

Terri shook her head. "No, no, I'm fine." She'd already said too much. "Thanks for listening."

She hung up before Ally could protest. Although the day was warm, chills raced through her.

She could think of a million reasons why this was a bad idea. So many reasons why she should get out now and walk away. Her job. His past. Their past. So many reasons.

Yet...the look in his eyes haunted her. She could no more walk away than she could stop breathing. She shook her head, quelling the thoughts that threatened to surface.

She was not falling in love with Clarke. She wasn't. She couldn't be.

Chapter Ten

Her IM buzzed with an urgent message from Kai. Terri read the words and went to her boss' office, unsure what could be causing him to need her right then. One glance into Kai's office told her the answer.

Harris, Clarke's old bass player, was splayed on Kai's couch like he owned the cushions. She gazed at the tall man with the thinning blond hair. He played his gaze over her face and body before grinning and turning his focus back to Kai.

Then Harris turned back. His mouth dropped open. She couldn't mistake the dawning recognition.

Her heart stopped. Did he recognize her in the "I recognize you from the Whammy Bar" sort of way or in the "you stalked the crap out of Clarke" kind of way?

Clarke followed right behind, almost running into a motionless Terri. "You wanted to see me, Kai...hi." He fixed his attention on Kai's guest before swallowing and turning to her.

For a minute there was nobody else in the room. His clear green eyes focused on hers, and she shivered despite the mild temperature in Kai's office. As Harris had done a moment ago, Clarke's uncertain gaze roved her body before meeting her eyes.

Harris rose, uncoiling his lanky body as he stood. He was bigger than the other two men and at least six inches taller than Terri. She had never noticed that when she was at the clubs, but the four inch heels she wore back then made up most of the difference.

"Hello, Clarke."

"Harris," Clarke said on a shocked exhalation of breath.

Harris had maintained his career since he left Attraction. When rock stopped paying the bills, he had gone back to his jazz/blues roots. She was aware of Harris's current blues focus, and also that he did a variety of things to stay afloat. As with most of the musicians of that era, his heyday was over, but he had so much talent that he would never go without work. She hadn't given the bass player more than a few seconds thought in the last few years. They hadn't been friends, but he had always been cordial. If not for Ally, Terri would have forgotten all about the man.

Of all the fallout from the band breakup, nothing had been worse than the schism between Clarke and Harris. They had once been good friends, but the friendship went south as Clarke's addictions spiraled out of control. Clarke had fired Harris as they were finalizing the mix for the album that turned out to be their last. Or Harris had quit. The rumor mills were divided on which was the truth. Whatever side people favored, the split had been a nasty affair. Harris had left the studio that day and to the best of her knowledge, exited Clarke's life.

"I didn't know you were coming in," Clarke said.

"Yeah? I knew you were here. My publicist reads the gossip columns, and you and Apposite get some press. I came anyway." Harris's voice was a low bass, a rumble deep in the stomach. The tone matched the instrument he played.

Clarke's hands moved over each other, and her heart lurched. He glanced at her again, fear in his eyes.

Terri took a step toward him. Harris had always rolled his eyes whenever she made a beeline for Clarke. He had cautioned her to leave Clarke alone, for both their sakes, long before the lawyers finished the job. If he remembered that she was Lynx, then he had the power to destroy their new relationship before it got off the ground.

Harris watched Clarke, his arms folded low across his body, hands resting on his elbows.

"I called you." Clarke shifted his palms up and out.

"Yeah." Harris's words were flat, with no inflection. "I got your messages."

The byplay was like watching two bulls ducking their heads and locking horns.

Clarke's glance flickered to Kai and then to Terri again. He paused, and she wondered if what he wanted to say was difficult in front of an audience.

"Clarke, spare me step number nine again, if you don't mind." Harris had an edge to his voice. "It's been a long time. Water under the bridge. I'm glad you're clean. We lose too many people to addiction in this business. I am not holding any grudges. Okay?" He glanced at Terri, but she couldn't interpret what he was trying to say.

Clarke's posture slumped for a moment before he met Harris's gaze again. The gesture took an eternity, but Harris held out his hand. The handshake was perfunctory, just two swift pumps, but a multitude of meanings lay behind the movement.

"So what the hell brings you here, man? Slumming?"

Harris extracted his hand and pointed to Kai. "This guy is interested in a side project Steve and I have going. An instrumental thing."

Clarke cocked an eyebrow at Kai, and she saw that swift stab of pain again before he masked it. "Yeah?"

In front of him was evidence of the shattered aftermath of the life he had destroyed with his own hands. He took it in with acceptance made greater by the touch of humility.

The bass player had no reason to forgive his former singer. Harris's name had been dragged through the mud after his firing. Clarke had given lengthy interviews and managed, without saying the words, to call Harris everything from power mad to greedy. Yet he had come to the office even being aware Clarke was part of the small label.

She watched the three men as they talked. Both Clarke and Harris had their arms crossed, their focus on Kai rather than each other.

Harris would be a fool to take his business to Apposite, with a takeover bid looming and an uncertain future, but he was here. Kai had to have offered the get-together to try and facilitate reconciliation between the former friends.

She had no reason to be there, and yet she stayed. Terri told herself she wanted to find out if Harris was going to spill the beans on her, but that was a lie.

Kai turned a pen over and over in his hand. Sun from his office windows made his straight hair glow blue black in its rays. "An instrumental album? With Steve Jacly?" Uncertainty and hope flew across his face. "We'd get some press for sure. You two still command an audience. But why us, and why not someone like Shatter Sound or Plausive? Your chances are better anywhere else."

"We've wanted to do this for a long time." Harris glanced at Clarke. "Studio work is fine, but it's been ages since I was creative."

"He's the best damned bass player in this country," Clarke said to Kai. "If they want to make music, let them. Maybe they could put one or two songs with lyrics on the CD. Steve sings."

At the mention of his old guitarist, pain crossed Clarke's face again, but he buried the emotion so fast she didn't think the other men were aware.

"Steve would rather go with a small label so we have the freedom to create. Our plan was to do a secret show at the Rumble to test out some new stuff. We'd get the word out on social media to draw a crowd. Something you guys are good at." He grinned at Kai. "I'm impressed." Harris paused. "The fans would freak if we did a few Attraction songs."

She started in surprise. Kai's mouth dropped open, his gaze going from Harris to Clarke, but he said nothing.

Clarke's mouth opened with no sound, and his shoulders slumped, his body curling inward before straightening. He stared at his former bass player. "Man…" His voice was strangled. "You can't be serious."

"As a matter of fact, I am. We are. Steve suggested a reunion." Harris studied Clarke for long seconds. "There's a lot of water under this bridge, but as long as you're sober, it's a practical move."

Kai's eyes had lit up with anticipation. "If you could add a song to the CD with Clarke, that would be a good item for the catalog too," he mused. "There's this guy who does great cover art."

****

Speechless, Clarke ran his hands through his hair. People who had known him back in the day would never believe he wouldn't have some witty comeback or smart comment. But those days, like the man, were gone.

He wondered if Terri had that howling sense of loneliness at three o'clock in the morning. Did she ever get so desperate to talk to someone that she flipped on her phone to search for people to chat with overseas? He hated calling his sponsor at those hours and only did so rarely when the desperation drove him to call the dude. A friendly female voice would have been better. Or a line and a bottle of Jack.

Nah. Terri August wasn't built that way. She wasn't consumed by self-doubt. He doubted she'd done anything inappropriate in her life. She was the perfect model citizen, always doing the right thing. She had things under control. Heat flooded him. In the important ways, she wasn't so controlled. She had allowed herself to come apart in his arms and show him a passionate side he had not imagined existed when they first met. He wasn't seeing anyone else—it didn't even enter his mind. He had no desire inside him for anyone but the intriguing female with stormy eyes and hair the color of gold and crimson.

You're a fucking poet, Masters.

He focused back on the office. Her body was tense through the loose-fitting yellow shell that only skimmed her breasts.

Don't stop, Clarke, don't stop.

Clarke fiddled with the pocket of his trousers, using his hand to shield his growing erection. The jingle of change was loud in a room gone silent, waiting for his answer. All eyes were on him. He cleared his throat again.

"Been a long time since I sang," he said. "I'm sure I would suck out there."

"You weren't Luciano Pavarotti back then." The bass of Harris's voice was pitched to the lowest part of his range. It was an intimidation tactic Clarke had seen the bass player use many times. Harris's focus went from Terri to Clarke, and Clarke was going to remove the man's eyes from his skull if he continued to devour Terri's body with them.

"Bastard." Clarke said, more of a growl than vowels and consonants put together.

"You just did music for the chicks." Harris glanced at Terri.

"Pot, meet kettle."

"Yep." Harris lapsed into silence, then directed his attention back to Clarke. "What do you think?"

Clarke's voice was unsteady when he spoke. "Um…sure, Harry. A reunion could help all of us. Lee won't do drums, though."

Harris waved a hand in dismissal. "Steve is married to a drummer. We can use Dana. I'm sure she has the songs memorized, and if she doesn't, she can improvise."

Longing and fear mingled within him. The last time he'd performed had been a small club in Vegas, and he was so bombed he fell off the stage. They'd had to refund most of the tickets. All he remembered was waking up, or coming to, in his crappy hotel room with a bill from his lawyer and a note that the guy quit. This was a chance to put things right and to make up for the wrongs he'd done to both Harris and Steve.

"Just a one-off thing, though," he said. "Rock and roll is my past. I left that life behind a few years ago. I'll do it for you and for what we once were. But we're old news, man. Do you really think people will show up?" Clarke tried not to show his excitement. He could make living amends to the band he'd screwed. Being there for them would make up for what happened in a way no apologies ever could.

"I'm sure they will. But you're the social media dude. Get word out there," Harris said with a challenge in his voice. "For old time's sake."

"Yeah. For old time's sake."

****

Clarke breathed in Terri's faint scent of clean linen mixed with the unmistakable tang of sex.

"What do you make of Harris's appearance?"

Clarke's hand stilled, and he moved back. Flipping on the nightstand light, he cupped her chin with one hand and urged her head up. She bit her lip before meeting his gaze again.

He had a nagging sense of missing something, a sensation that had only intensified since the meeting in Kai's office. He wondered if being around Harris had reminded her of what Clarke really was. An addict. A failed singer. A man with little to recommend him. Maybe she didn't want people to realize she was having sex with him. Maybe this Clarke wasn't good enough for Terri August.

Maybe, maybe, maybe, he mocked himself. If he wanted her to tell him what she was thinking, he should just ask her. He would, but not yet. He hoped she would do it without prodding.

"I think Harris is practical. He's aware he's going to get the kind of individual attention from Apposite that he wouldn't get at another label. He is also aware that Attraction playing the Rumble is going to generate the kind of buzz you couldn't buy with any amount of money. Even on a Monday night."

She reached up and combed the hair back off his forehead.

He closed his eyes. "Yeah, that makes sense. Terri..."

"Yeah?"

He hoped she could hear the sincerity in his voice. "I didn't know. I didn't understand how much I craved the feel of a woman. I wasn't aware how much I missed having someone in my life until you came along. I thought I didn't want one woman. I mean..."

He broke off as her fingers continued against his head, pressing against his temples and then running down the length of his jaw.

"Do you ever feel despair, Terri? Do you ever wake up in the middle of the night so lonely you feel like screaming?"

Her gaze slid to a point beyond him. "Yes. But as bad as life gets, I try to always remember what I learned reading CoDA literature. I think I was reading CoDA, anyway. They said nothing is solved at three in the morning."

He studied her with a quizzical expression. "Co-dependent literature? Why would you read that?"

She turned away, not meeting his gaze. "It never hurts to learn things."

He pulled her on top of him so her butt rested against his rising arousal. "Tick tock, tick tock, Tyris August." He grasped her shoulders, his palms clammy. Sweat bloomed on his face and body, evidence of a fear he couldn't control. Butterflies danced in his stomach, bile rising in his throat.

"What?"

"Your wheels are spinning so fast they're audible in the next county. You're wondering if I would have been interested in any woman who liked me." When she flushed, he frowned. "True?"

She opened her mouth and then hesitated. He tensed, both dreading and anticipating what she might say.

"Well, yeah, I guess I did wonder that."

His sharp intake of breath was loud in the quiet room.

"I'm sorry, Clarke, it's just…"

He put her from him and rose from the bed. With his back to her, he stood there, his head slumped and his hands clenched.

The bed gave next to him, and then she wrapped her arms around his waist. He jerked but didn't reject her touch. Slowly his shoulders relaxed, and he slipped his hands into hers.

"Maybe in the beginning I wanted the attention, but not now. I don't want someone just to have someone. I want you. We had a rough start," he said, his voice shaky. "But I'm not going out with anyone else, and I hope you aren't either. You're not a body to me, Terri. I'm so attracted to you my mind spins."

She pressed a kiss against his spine and began trailing kisses down the column. "Me too, Clarke. I'm not interested in anyone else. Thank you. That had to be hard to learn."

He turned and tugged her up so she was standing. Cupping her face with his hands, he studied her. "Yeah, it was. But I don't ever want you to be less than honest with me. I've spent too long hiding from life while pretending to live that I want the truth. This time I want a relationship that is grounded. I want things real."

He wanted to shake her and get her to tell him what was on her mind. As he watched, her eyes shadowed but then cleared. Even though it killed him to wait, he was going to let her come to him. Her truth was hers to tell, and forcing her wouldn't work.

"Reality, sure. I'm not always good about saying what I feel, but I'll try."

He kissed her, skimming her lips with his tongue. "Hmm. There's something I'd like to explore right now." He pressed her back onto the bed and straddled her.

Clarke made love to her slowly, his hands and mouth working her until she was in a fever pitch, clutching at his shoulders, his hair, and lower, circling his member with her hand.

"Now. It's got to be now."

After putting a condom on, he pushed inside her and began a slow rhythm. Terri met his thrusts with a deep movement of her body, taking him all the way in.

"Oh, babe, babe," he cried on a hoarse shout as she made a mewling sound, rippling in orgasm. "I'm coming."

They lay tangled in his sheets, sated and drowsy. An overwhelming rush of emotion swept over him, something unfamiliar and warm, like he was coming home.

"I might love...you..." he muttered under his breath even as sleep caught at him.

From a distance he heard her ask, "What did you say?"

But dreams claimed Clarke, and he didn't reply.

Chapter Eleven

"Can we survive another month?" Kai paced back and forth in the space in front of her desk until she wanted to scream at him to stop. He held a file folder in his hand, holding on to it so tightly the manila threatened to tear at the seam. New worry lines bracketed his mouth and eyes. He had glasses on, and his hair was tied with a leather thong at the base of his neck.

Her uneasiness had to show in the tightness of her shoulders. "I'm not sure. Things are going to be close."

He flopped into her guest chair. Sighing, he pressed his fingertips to his temples, making circular motions. "Shit. Do what you can. If there's bills you can let slide, go ahead. I…I have to think about what to do."

"I will."

"Yeah. Oh, before I forget." He tossed the contents of the file folder onto her desk. Inside were three renditions of Clarke's cover. That morning in her office seemed a lifetime away.

She traced first one drawing and then another. The stylized artist leaped off the picture in his intensity, the multi-colored, swirling background behind him.

"Kai." She regarded her boss. "He wouldn't let me see them. These are remarkable."

A ghost of a grin flitted across his face at her

statement. "Which one do you like better?"

She finally chose the one with strongest primary colors. The picture evoked images of jungle cats and fierce thunderstorms, a leashed power that suited the speed-metal sound of the band.

"This one." She handed the chosen piece of paper back to him.

"I agree." He took all three versions, placing her favorite on top, and slid them back into the manila file folder. "You're sleeping together." He gave her a questioning look that added to the statement.

She contemplated how to phrase her answer and then went for honesty. "Yes. Is that a problem?" She steepled her fingers, her heart thudding as she waited for his reply.

Kai chuckled. "No, although I wouldn't have expected it of you. You and Clarke are a…surprise." He held up his hand. "What you do with your personal life is your concern. I'm a bit startled, though."

"Why?"

He ran his hand over his hair before peering at her under the frameless lenses of his glasses. "To be candid, you are very different people. He is a friend, and I love him, but I wouldn't have pictured the two of you together."

"I'm not wild enough for Clarke Masters. Is that what you're saying?"

He laughed, his body rippling with the sound. "I'm glad that chip on your shoulder isn't quite gone."

She ducked her head to hide her reaction. "Sorry, Kai."

He crossed around behind her desk and put his hands on her shoulders. "I've worked with you for five years, and I've never once seen you drop your mask and live in the moment. You are very careful, with your emotions and your words. You let nobody in. The only joy you get from life is cooking. Not that I don't appreciate your meals." He patted his stomach. "You take things seriously, which is admirable, but you never allow yourself to have fun or let your guard down. You don't let people in. I know little about you besides what everyone else does. I did not anticipate that you would have allowed yourself to be vulnerable enough to be in a relationship. I was wrong, and to be honest, Terri, I am glad I was."

She didn't tell him how dangerous she was when she let down her guard. She didn't say what happened when she allowed her child to run wild. She didn't tell him that her whole adult life had been a careful construct, designed to keep her emotions safe.

"I'm working on it." She choked out the words like bitter fruit.

"I always suspected there was more to you than met the eye. Don't throw up your defenses. You can freeze men out with that lowered stare of yours. Try to resist falling back into that habit. I'm happy for you."

How would Kai react to the news that she had been an obsessed groupie? That the only reason she got by in the world was by not allowing herself to let people in? She doubted he'd be so interested in her getting together with his friend if he was familiar with the whole truth.

"Do you think he's ready?" The words ripped out of her.

He studied her for a long moment. "Are you? I assumed you weren't interested in relationships."

She fiddled with a pen, wanting to confide in Kai. Terri reviewed her list of friends. She needed some new ones and also needed to nurture the girlfriends she did have. Ally was the only one she trusted, and Ally had her own life, her own romance. She should have relationships outside of Clarke. She wanted to have fun that didn't start and end in bed with him. She would check if that discounted coupon for a cake decorating class she'd bought was still good.

"I think so. I'm just not sure I'm the right woman."

"The right woman for what?"

Terri started. She hadn't heard Clarke come into the office. "We, uh, decided on a picture for the cover," she said, her voice shaking. "I was wondering if I was the right person to keep things going."

"Did you?" His eyes were narrowed, and he was glaring at Kai as if he wanted to tear strips out of the Asian man.

"This one." Kai took the picture out of the folder and handed it to Clarke.

Clarke glanced down. "Yeah, that's my favorite too." He glared at Kai again and then flicked his glance to Terri.

"I didn't realize when I hired you that I was matchmaking." Kai clapped Clarke on the shoulder. "I'll leave you to it." He bowed and took his leave.

Clarke studied the picture he still held in his hand.

"He told me the same thing." She willed the dark pain out of his eyes.

"What?" His lips were compressed.

"Not to fuck up. He didn't phrase the words that way, but that's what he meant. I told him about us. He already knew. Should we be telling people? I mean, work colleagues…"

He strode across the room and yanked her against him. Bending her down so her torso was over the muscled strength of his forearm, he kissed her. Her door was open. The entire office witnessed the smooch.

Her ears and cheeks burning, she half expected applause when he let her up. All noise had stopped from outside. There was no conversation, no clacking of keys, and no sounds of the copier or any of the background hum that made up the office's daily routine.

"Well," she said, out of breath, "I guess that answers that question."

"Damned right it does. I'll put a full-page announcement in any magazine if you want me to."

Her cheeks blazed even hotter. In that moment she understood she was still in love with him. She'd never stopped, even after all the intervening years. "That won't be necessary. Clarke?"

"Yeah?"

She crossed the office and shut the door. The people on the other side would think a lot of things about what they could do behind a closed door, but for once she didn't care.

She had too much to say and no way to say it. The truth beat at her chest like a trapped bird. She ignored it, seizing on the first safe topic she could think of. Safe for her, anyway. "Tell me what happened with Harris."

He sputtered a snort that turned into a cough. He stared at her with incomprehension, clearly expecting a different topic. "Harris? Why?"

Harris had said to her, "I remember you," in passing, telling her that he recalled her entire history with Clarke. She wasn't sure why Harris hadn't told Clarke; maybe Harris assumed his old vocalist knew. Now she was curious about Harris in a way she had never been back when she was obsessed with Clarke.

Clarke was still wheezing from his coughing fit. "I was a jerk." His voice was faint.

She nodded. "I get that. But I've been watching you guys, and there's a bond there. I want the story from you."

He half turned and began tapping his fingers against his thigh in a rhythmic beat, but saying nothing. "Babe, you're asking a lot." He sighed. "It's something I'd rather forget, but damn, they got this crap out of me in rehab, and you deserve to know."

To her relief, he stopped drumming on his body. With a swift motion, he gestured to her, holding out his hand. "I was appalling. I was such an ass."

Her fingers curled around his, accepting his touch. He took her hand and squeezed.

Terri spoke into the silence. "There's a philosopher that Kai quotes. I have no idea what his name is. He says 'those who do not remember the past are doomed to repeat it.' You remembered. You learned. That's all I need."

****

He wanted to kiss her until they were both screaming their desire for each other.

Yeah, good move. Make love in the office. Add that to his list of crimes.

The hardening of his penis told him his body didn't give a shit about getting caught, this time for all the right reasons. He could feel the soft warmth of her breasts under his hands, their peaks reddening until she sighed in his arms. He would bury his face in the sweet, subtle floral scent of her unbound hair as he caressed her. He could almost feel her shuddering and could imagine those little mewling cries she made when she got excited.

He had stiffened and was staring at her when she said, "Clarke?"

He blinked. Their hands were locked together, white marks visible where he had been gripping too hard.

He relaxed his grip, still caught in the fierce need she evoked from him. "Sorry. All you have to do to turn me on is breathe. Right. Harris."

Much of the last ten years was hazy, but this incident was burned in his mind. It might as well have happened yesterday, so clear were the images. Clarke let memory take him, speaking out loud to Terri while lost in his own reveries.

"The album was almost done, and I decided to go to the Whammy Bar, which was nothing new. I practically lived there. That led to one of the all-night drug orgies that happened in Laurel Canyon. You remember those?" If she nodded or showed any sign of recognition, he had no idea; he was so caught by memories. "There was a pack of rich Whammy Bar guys who had tons of money and lived to party with rock stars. I got bored and invited several women back to my townhouse to continue the fun."

Her gray eyes were hooded, revealing nothing.

He took a deep breath and continued. "That same morning I was scheduled to be at the studio to go over the final mix. The band and half a dozen record executive honchos were there. All we needed to do was put the finishing touches on the mixes, and the album would be good to go. I never showed."

He wondered if she had read about the incident in the news, but then dismissed the idea. His sordid exploits wouldn't have interested her.

"Fucking doorbell wouldn't stop ringing. The buzz finally woke me up. I had three girls with me and kept rolling into soft bodies no matter where I turned. A thousand elves were pounding on my head, and the sound filled the townhouse. The light was coming through the blinds, so it had to be midday. I didn't have any conception what day it was. All I knew was that someone was pissing me off by ringing my bell. I swore into the intercom and told the moron on the other end to 'go the fuck away, whoever you are.' My head was pounding, my mouth was so dry my lips were chapped, and there was blood down the front of my face."

He heard her draw in a breath, but he didn't shift his focus.

"The girls kept giggling and pawing at me. A crane couldn't have gotten me up at that point. I still had my hand on the buzzer when a voice crackled through the intercom again. 'Get up, you worthless asshole,' Harris said. I told him to fuck off. Then my cell started ringing, and even as fucked up as I was, I had to answer. I picked up my phone but said nothing. After a minute of silence and a deep sigh, Harris continued. 'Screw up your life all you want, *buddy*, but we've got an album to finish. I don't give a shit who you dick around with, but this is your job. You want to throw your life all away on blow and booze, that's fine with me. Just don't take me down with you.' He was bitter, angry, each word like acid, especially the 'buddy' one. I hadn't been his buddy for years. We'd been friends since high school, but I was nobody's friend by then." He paused again, taking a drink of water. His hand was shaking, the liquid waving in the glass.

Terri was far away, seeming to be lost in her own musings.

"I told him I didn't report to him. He reminded me I reported to the label and I'd better get my ass down to the studio in an hour, or he'd be back for me. There was no getting around it. I got rid of the women and tried to get ready. I could only bear my face in the mirror for a second. I was pale and sweaty as hell, even after a shower, my eyes were red, and my complexion was blotchy. Then I threw up, heaving up stomach bile and nothing else.

"I'd left my keys in the car ignition. I didn't even remember getting to the townhouse and was relieved that my car was in its space. As I drove, I started to get mad. Harris was a good-for-nothing bass player. Who was he to talk to me like that? I didn't need any two-bit musician lecturing me on my duties. By the time I got to the place, I was furious. I threw up again, but my stomach held nothing, so all that came up was water. I felt like hell. I wanted to turn around and go home, but I'd exhausted my excuses. I'd just agree to whatever they suggested and be done with my job."

His mouth was as parched as it had been on that day. Clarke took another swallow of water, but the liquid did nothing to ease the despair swirling inside him. This was going to be too much for her. She wouldn't understand.

"Harris and the others glared at me when I came in. One of the label executives muttered something like 'look what the cat dragged in.' I wanted to snap at him, but I was trying to stop from barfing again. When I was confident I wasn't going to hurl, I shouted at Harris to fuck off and that I was giving him the boot. Nobody said anything for a minute, so I repeated that he was fired and told him to get out."

Terri spoke for the first time. "I read something about that. The papers said Harris went for you and that Steve and the label had to separate you guys? That you threatened to break Harris's hands? They said you tried to karate chop him."

He opened his mouth, but she was still speaking.

"I heard that Steve tried to talk to both of you, but neither of you were listening. I don't recall all the details, but after that fight Harris walked out, and that was the end of Attraction."

He nodded. "We broke up. The other guys refused to have anything to do with me. Our band was over the minute I set foot in that studio." He remembered how nauseated he'd been that day. The days like that one deterred him when he thought picking up a drink was a good idea.

She whistled, the sound soft and low. "No wonder he didn't return your calls," she said, her eyes focused on a spot on the wall.

"I wouldn't have either. I was a dick." When she said nothing, Clarke sighed. "We should open the door. I think you need some fresh air." Self-loathing dug into his psyche. He was sure she couldn't wait to be clear of him. His past was appalling, and she was so straight, so perfect.

"You're doing that thing again," she said, even as she did what he suggested and wrenched her office door open. People scattered where they had been huddled in groups. Clarke caught Sunshine's look of interest and winked at her, although the gesture was far from what he was feeling. Their shared secretary grinned before turning her attention back to her computer.

"What?" He studied Terri, trying to make sense out of her statement.

"Assuming you know what I'm going to say next." Her eyes were shadowed, but her voice was bright.

"Which was?" He waited for her answer, hoping his eagerness didn't show.

"That was then, this is now. You're not that man. None of us are the same people we were back then."

"Thanks. The truth wasn't too much for you?" A surge of relief so great he nearly went to the floor rushed over him.

She paused, pursing her lips, and then shook her head. "It's an ugly story, but that's all. A tale, part of your history, but not who you are today."

She appeared to want to say something else, but the phone rang before she spoke any further words. Whatever she had been about to say was lost in that moment.

He told himself he didn't know what he had been hoping she would say.

Chapter Twelve

He could always tell when people knew who he was. Expectation always shone in their eyes, like he should greet them as an old friend. Usually he had to struggle to place them, and often he just faked acknowledgment.

Today was no exception. He studied the woman in front of him without speaking.

"Aren't you Clarke Masters?" She pointed toward him.

The sparsely attended club was in Ontario, a city about fifty miles from Los Angeles. Clarke wondered why he'd bothered to make the drive. They weren't in Hollywood, where the mere act of leaving a restaurant could result in a blurb on the gossip sites within minutes. He had come because he'd heard good things about the band and he needed to start taking his A&R duties seriously. So far the two opening acts had been dreadful, and unless the headliner lived up to their publicity, this had been a wasted trip.

The dark-haired woman who faced him was pretty, or had been once upon a time. Her gamine quality had doubtless been appealing when she was younger, but the lines and furrows on her face placed her around forty. She could be younger, if she was someone who had done, or was still doing, a lot of cocaine.

Clarke cursed his tricky memory when the woman

didn't appear familiar. She had probably been a groupie frequenting the same clubs he did. He might have slept with her—although he generally preferred blondes—but anything was possible.

He removed his earplugs and held out his hand. "I'm Clarke." He tried to strike a polite tone despite his lack of interest. It never hurt to be polite.

"Lola," she said, flipping her long, curly hair over her shoulder before taking his hand. "I used to date Jake Lane."

Jake Lane was a guitarist for the flamboyant vocalist known only as Imran. Attraction opened for them in the early days, in a US and Latin America tour. Clarke had no idea what became of the man. Like so many others, Jake had faded from Clarke's life.

"Jake, sure." He returned the gesture with a brief grasp of his palm. He would never be able to replace those missing spans of time, but he could ensure that he didn't lose any more.

"What are you up to?" She gestured around the club, her gaze darting around before flitting back to Clarke and away again. She was jittery, shifting from one foot to another, and a sheen of sweat shone on her face, even through the heavy makeup. He recognized the signs of someone who still enjoyed her recreational drugs. Her gaze met his, and she spoke again. "Rumor has it you went to rehab and got clean. Congratulations."

"I did. A little over two years. I'm doing A&R now. Small label called Apposite Records."

The woman's eyebrows shot up, and her mouth opened in an O of surprise. The crowd noise was dimmer between sets, but they still had to raise their voices to hear each other.

"Apposite? Really? I used to be friends with someone who was there. She must be gone."

"Who?" His feeling of dread intensified. This woman and Terri might be about the same age, if the deep lines in her face were due to drug use rather than age. Kai had mentioned that Terri went to the Whammy Bar once upon a time. He stuck his hands deep into the pockets of his black slacks. He barely suppressed tapping his foot, contenting himself with moving his toes inside his sneakers.

"Terri August."

He sucked in his breath at the mention of Terri's name. *She must be gone.* The woman, whose name he had already forgotten, had said the words without hesitation.

"She's still there." He wished he had a cigarette, anything to give him something to do. He started flexing his hands against the fabric of his pants pockets. "She's a one-woman office dynamo. We're friends."

The woman's bright red lips pursed, and her jaw slackened. "You and Terri? You're kidding."

The incredulity in her tone sent arrows of pain through his chest. A sense of failure, of not being enough, washed over him. He thought he'd lost that stinging sensation, but maybe he never would. "Not kidding. We work together, and we have the same interests. Why wouldn't we hang out?"

"I guess there's a statute of limitations on restraining orders." She said the words almost to herself. Almost, but not quite. Her mouth tightened until the lines in her cheeks stood out as white slashes.

Clarke stared at her. The back of his neck prickled.

After an uncomfortable silence he found his voice. "Restraining orders? She didn't like me much but not enough to take out a restraining order on me. We never met until I started working at the label." Of course if they had, he wouldn't have remembered, but the Terri he'd first encountered would have thrown something like that at him. The Terri he had in his life would have told him.

She laughed. The sound was loud, with a touch of cruelty. Clarke wondered what kind of friends they had been back in the day.

"Not her. You. Hmm. Maybe your warning didn't get to restraining order." No mistaking the meanness now. Her hands clenched, and her eyes narrowed until they were mere slits. She studied him and then swept her head from side to side, her long hair waving with the movement. "You called her...huh, what was it again?"

She paused again, an act Clarke knew was for effect. Part of him wanted to grab her and shake the story out of her. The other part wanted her to shut up and never finish.

"Oh, right. I think the term was 'my little stalker.' Or maybe your exact words were, hang on, 'my little Maine stalker.' "

"My what?" He struggled to keep his casual stance, shifting from foot to foot in agitation. Unease settled in his stomach, the persistent nagging feeling that he'd missed something this entire time surging to the surface and leaving him breathless.

The woman glanced toward the stage area where people were buzzing with activity setting up the headlining band before turning back to him. She studied him and shook her head. "Your stalker. Don't you remember? The underage blonde who haunted the Whammy Bar? The one who lingered after closing time again and again until you paid some attention to her? The one who wouldn't leave you alone afterward? Will Bevison and I used to laugh about it."

He'd had his share of women who haunted him after the fact. Usually a few curt words and a brush off was all he needed, but if not, he had people who handled those things.

"Stalker?" He searched his faded memory for details of what Terri's former friend was talking about. She was telling the truth. The glint in her eyes and the malevolent glee on her face showed she was enjoying this.

"You said 'groupies know their place, or they know where the door is.' Terri didn't."

He shook his head, running his hand over his forehead.

The woman—Lana, Lara?—was still studying him with an air of anticipation. Clarke set his soda down. He couldn't stay there. The headliner hadn't come on yet, but he had to get out, had to get away from the flaying sting of Terri's ex-friend's words.

He stood up and waved at her. "I have to go." Pushing through the sparse crowd, he stumbled outside in the night air, barely aware of his surroundings.

His paperwork was well organized, courtesy of a series of assistants. Everything had been labeled and filed and stored in his office in his Glendale home. If this woman was telling the truth, he should find something in there.

****

The continuous pounding roused Terri out of deep sleep. The knocks were staccato and rhythmic, three beats, then one, then silence. Then again. She recognized Clarke's knock, but that made no sense. He was in Ontario at a gig.

She was rumpled and unkempt from sleep, wearing a T-shirt and drawstring pants. Her hair was a disaster, and she reached up a hand to smooth the strands. Clarke knocked again in the same pattern.

When he was inside, he started pacing.

"Clarke?" she asked uncertainly. "What are you doing here? You're supposed to be in Ontario at that show..." She peered at the clock over her TV. Eleven o'clock. The band hadn't even gone on yet. Her puzzlement deepened.

He stopped walking back and forth and gave her a sharp stare. He had a folder in his hands, a manila one with a label across the top. Papers were stuck in the folder at right angles from the tan file.

"Clarke?" Her gaze fell on the file. She couldn't read what was written, but she didn't need to. The folder was old, with bent corners. Their office folders were black, so any hope that he carried something from the office came and went in the moment she breathed the notion in and back out.

"Why didn't you tell me?" He turned the folder up and toward her.

Her name leaped from the tab, mocking her. *Tyris August* was in neat Courier typeface, saying everything she hadn't had the courage to admit.

"Tell you what?" The quiver in her voice matched the trembling of her hands. She clamped her teeth together before the chattering became obvious.

143

Terri flipped on the living room light and then flicked it off again. The light was too stark for the truth. Instead, she opted for a table lamp she rarely used. Her hands wobbled when she turned the light on, and she dropped onto the sofa in the hopes sitting down would conceal the shake in her body. She might have been standing, naked, on a snow-covered mountain.

"This is no time for games."

His voice was flat and emotionless. She had gotten used to his lilt, the pleasure emanating from within when he spoke to her. This harsh quality was new and unwelcome—and her fault.

"I am not playing games."

He raked one hand through his hair, misery etched into the downturned lips and creased brow. Lowering his arms, he stared at her, and the pain in his eyes made her want to go and hold him.

"I tried all the way here, and I don't remember you." He gestured to the file folder. "You would think I would. Tyris is an unusual name." He tossed the dossier onto her coffee table. The damning folder skittered across, spilling its contents like a dropped purse.

Moonlight glinted off his strong body, casting shadows throughout the room. He began pacing, back and forth across the short hallway between her kitchen and dining room, until she wanted to scream at him to halt.

"An old friend of yours with dark hair and bright red lips moved to Ontario. Remember who I mean? Did you know that? I use the term 'friend' with sarcasm."

She jerked upright. That could only be one person. "Do you mean Lola?"

He nodded. "That sounds right."

"No. She went to Fullerton, not Ontario. She...oh..."

She was even more ashamed of herself for not telling him the truth as soon as they'd become friends. If not then, she should have told him after they were lovers. She had owed that to a man who fought his demons and won. She needed to reveal her own shameful past, and instead she had run from the idea. She had made him believe she was some perfect person, when she was no better than he was.

"She told me about our past. My little stalker. God, I feel like an idiot."

He looked so distraught that she cursed herself again for lying to him. Good or bad, come what may, she would no longer hide this truth. She had been a coward. "Lola told you? I bet she loved that. Your exact words were 'my little Maine stalker,' if you want to get technical." She ached to touch him, but his forbidding expression stayed her hand. She had no idea what he was thinking.

He sat down on the arm of her couch. "Oh yeah, she did. She enjoyed every minute. I'm betting you're not friends these days."

Terri snorted, shaking her head. "You'd win that bet. After our blowup happened, I wasn't a good club partner. You had me barred from the Whammy Bar, and she wanted to be with the bands. We were just club buddies anyway, and she dropped me like a hot potato when my usefulness ran out. I was a mess, and she didn't have the time or the desire to console me. That wasn't my purpose."

He let out a harsh laugh. "Some friend." He studied the folder. "I want to say I remember a little now. My

Claire Davon

assistant put a picture in the file, and the photo was a
little familiar. You are so different now."

She searched for the right words, something to
mitigate the damage, but her mind was a blank. She
twined her hands around each other over and over again
before forcing herself to stop. "You liked blondes, so I
became a platinum blonde. You preferred scantily clad
women, so I went to the Hollywood Boulevard stores
that had dresses that showed a lot of skin. I chose a
different name, Lynx, like the cat. You liked lots of
makeup, so Lola did me up. She was a makeup artist
and slathered the paint on."

"She still does."

"I'm not surprised." Her heart was pounding and
the shaking replaced by a thin sheen of perspiration.
Her mouth had the bitter, acrid taste of fear. "Who
wants to be remembered that way? I was sure, in my
stupid girlish naiveté, that once you met me, you would
fall in love with me and want me for your girlfriend.
When you didn't, I believed if I kept trying, you would
understand how terrific I was and change your mind. I
was rude and horribly pushy. I hate remembering that
time in my life. I had no boundaries. I'm sorry, Clarke.
I should have told you."

He rose from the couch again, his movements
slow. He started pacing again, like a caged animal.

"The file had a certified letter from an attorney
who told you if you didn't cease and desist harassing
me, I was going to get a restraining order. I didn't send
the note or ask for it to be sent. My assistant must have
wanted you off my back. Maybe I asked her to get rid
of you. I don't remember. I used the same law firm as
the label, but the person on the letterhead wasn't my

attorney."

She breathed out, the knot in her belly loosening at the knowledge that she hadn't pushed him that far. "I researched the firm on the letter later on. The attorney who sent the letter didn't exist. I clung to that hope that I wouldn't get a restraining order summons and was relieved when I didn't. It took me almost a year to stop worrying. Still…" She took a deep breath, shaking her head. "Have you ever read *Pride and Prejudice*, Clarke?"

He snorted, a touch of amusement turning up his lips before they settled into firm lines again. "A stripper I used to do blow with was in love with the dude in the miniseries, so we had that version on a couple of times when we were doing drugs. It's a chick thing. Not my kind of book."

She nodded. "Colin Firth. He was the 'dude in the miniseries.' I have a beat-to-heck paperback somewhere that is dog-eared and underlined to death. I identified with Mr. Darcy."

"Not the woman? Liz or Lizzy or whatever her name was?" He continued to study her and then waved his hand, the motion stopping halfway before he let his arm fall back to his side.

She swallowed before continuing.

"Nope, Mr. Darcy all the way. You have to understand I was hurt and embarrassed. At first I clung to righteous anger and told anyone who would listen how misunderstood I was. Most people stopped answering my calls and emails. Lola was the first to go, but she wasn't the last. I hadn't been here long enough to build up friendships and goodwill to carry me through something like that. My club buddies vanished, and my reason for going to the clubs also disappeared. I held on to my anger for a few months, and then I was sickened at my actions. It took me a little while to recognize how much I was to blame. Anyway, Mr. Darcy. He says toward the end of *Pride and Prejudice* something to the effect of his behavior being unpardonable. I think the line is 'I cannot think of it without abhorrence.' "

She stopped, all the recriminations she'd beaten herself up with over the last ten years settling on her psyche like a stone. Terri forced herself to continue.

"I'm sorry for everything. For being your stalker and for not telling you. For holding the past against you. You were rough with my feelings at the time, but in the end the fault was mine. I was pushy and out of control. You would have had every right to get a restraining order."

"That's enough with the apologies." His voice was low and monotone. His face was set and hard, the lines apparent even through the dimmer light of the table lamp. "For my part, I'm sorry too. Not because of the ninth step, but for me. I do owe you an amends. I had no business sleeping with someone I didn't love." He glanced at her and then back away. "What aren't you telling me? You're leaving something out."

The words seared her, dread curling through her body. She hesitated, not wanting to tell him the rest. This was bad enough.

First blankness and then surprise and understanding crossed his face. "You were a virgin."

She bit her lip, nodded. "Yes."

He rose and began pacing again. "Was the sex good at least?"

It would be a kindness to lie. She could save his ego by telling him how wonderful their first time had been. But there was no point in that. She had come this far, and to give him anything other than the truth would do both of them a disservice. She didn't know if they could survive this, but for sure they wouldn't if she continued to lie.

"You wanted things I'd only read about in magazines. Finally, you just put a condom on, ordered me to spread my legs, and entered me. You said to get this over with. You said you were on the verge of demanding a blow job, but you doubted I'd be any good at that. After you had come, you said if I wanted to play in the big leagues, I'd better learn some tricks to keep a man interested. I assumed if I could improve and get you back into bed, I would knock your socks off. I stalked you, you had that part right, but you didn't want a repeat performance. I watched porn to learn, but you didn't care. You told me you were Clarke Masters and you could, and did, get far superior lovers."

"Did I know?"

She shook her head.

"It's all clear now. That's why you freaked this time when we made love."

"Yes." She took heart in the fact that he said "made love" and not "had sex."

He went to her. For a moment she thought he was going to put his arms around her, but instead he knelt. Taking her hands, he stared at her. Their eyes almost level, sorrow and pain etched in his green depths.

"I have to ask, Terri. Was our relationship because of what happened? Because of your crush on me? Did you see it as a way of fulfilling your old fantasy?"

She gasped, her eyes widening. Of all the things she had imagined he would say when confronted with this truth, that was the last one that crossed her mind. His face was set, his eyes blazing with intensity. Terri wanted to look away but was compelled to keep her gaze on his.

The silence went on a beat, then two. Too long. Many words crowded her mind as she tried to find the right ones. "Clarke, no. Oh my God, no. I wanted to keep my distance, but I couldn't. You're like a beacon in the night. That's how bright you shine. There was no resisting you. I didn't get involved with you because of what happened, as some sort of weird proof that I'd been right ten years ago. The opposite, if anything at all. I was sure you would hate me if you knew the truth."

He let out a breath. Releasing her hands, he stood. "I…" He held out his hands in a helpless gesture. "Honestly, Terri, I couldn't tell you what I'm feeling right now. Part of me wants to go, but the bigger part of me can't imagine leaving this apartment. Not with you in it." He pressed her into him until she was almost smothered by the fabric of his shirt.

She sighed and wrapped around him, the heat of their bodies mingling. "I'm sorry." As words went, they felt wholly inadequate, but she had nothing else.

"No secrets, Tyris. We can't exist with them. If we've got any shot, you have to promise me."

"Yes, Clarke. I swear."

Then he released her and stepped back. "I am serious, though, babe. This…" He pointed to the manila file folder, which was still spilled across her coffee table. "This is huge. It explains a lot, but man…" He paused. He was going to end things with her; that had to be what he was about to do. After everything that happened, she wouldn't be surprised. She deserved that.

"I…I was raised to be fair-minded." She stuttered over the statement. "Hippies, free love, live and let live, all those throwbacks to the sixties."

When he nodded, she swallowed and continued.

"All my life I was taught that nothing was impossible and I should go for what I wanted. I'd had a crush on you from videos and interviews. I didn't know you, of course, but that didn't matter. I'd always intended to move out here. You were a bonus, but not the reason. Still I made the most of it. I found out where you hung out and went there. I got myself introduced to you. I found out where you were going to be and made it a point to show up there. You really have no recollection of any of this?"

Clarke didn't speak, and she wondered if he was about to lie. He shook his head. A stab of sympathy went through her. How tragic to have large chunks of your memory gone forever.

"I…" She faltered again. "I can give you all the sordid details if you want, but it hurts my soul to remember how idiotic I was. When I still wouldn't stop, that's when I got this." She pointed to the table where the folder still lay. "The threat of a restraining order was a shock of icy cold water."

She plucked the folder from the coffee table and extracted the letter. She knew the contents by heart, of course. "I freaked. I was furious, angry, and hated you and everything else. I couldn't go back to the Whammy Bar since you'd banned me. Then I ditched my former life. I went back to school, got an MBA, and went into business. Rock clubs and rock stars were just extravagant fools, and you were the worst of all. That's what I told myself. I didn't need to stay in music, and yet I did, so once again I was lying. I tried to hate everything about you. I made you the bad guy. Clarke, I…"

She swallowed again. "I was glad when your life went to hell and everyone turned their backs on you. I'm not proud of that. Then you came back into my life, and I couldn't hold those beliefs for long. All the reasons I had a crush on you as a teenager were still there. I became aware of how unfair I'd been—how awful. I'm so ashamed of the way I behaved, and I never want to be that person again." *I will never be that person again.*

His eyes darkened to forest green. "Wow. I've never met that person. Or maybe I did. I drove people to do a lot of crazy things with my actions. I am sure you were terrible, but I was as well. This, all this"—he pointed first to himself and then to her—"we weren't to prove something to yourself? We're for real?"

"We're real. I had a fantasy of you back then, a picture in my mind grafted onto the reality of you. I gave you all sorts of motives and belief systems that had nothing to do with you. I had ridiculous notions of men. This time, I got to know the complex, amazing man you are. I was lucky enough to meet the real Clarke Masters. You're a good man, and I'm happy we met a second time." She touched his arm. "Does that make any sense?"

She waited as he swallowed, his eyes searching hers.

He placed his opposite hand over hers, pressing their palms together. "It makes a lot of sense." He snorted, the sound harsh in the quiet night. "You were supposed to be perfect—nothing could get to you. This is a revelation. You're human, just like me. You just kicked yourself off a pedestal, babe."

She sighed in relief when he urged her forward into his arms again. His slow, steady heartbeat and the exhalation of his breath against her forehead coursed through her. Nothing had ever been so right. At that time, she had experienced thwarted passion and hurt anger. Her past feelings had been a child's fantasy, a teenager's dream. This time the emotions were deeper, the feelings of an adult.

"I'm fine with that."

She had imagined she loved him ten years ago, but that was obsessive nonsense. That was a teenage crush on an unattainable man who didn't exist. This time her love was real. She loved the man he was and the man he would be. Even when she didn't like everything about him, she loved him.

He lifted his head and grazed a kiss across her nose. "Come on. Let's go to bed."

Relief flooding her, Terri nodded.

Chapter Thirteen

"Where are we going?"

His smile was impish. "You'll see."

Clarke parked on a side street several blocks above Melrose Boulevard. They walked in silence to the bustling street, dodging the press of humanity thick along the narrow sidewalk. He watched her as they moved down the street, wondering if she was aware they were approaching the art galleries in the area.

"I like to find out what people are doing." He flexed his hand in hers. "The street makes me feel alive."

They paused in front of the window display of one of the best known, prestigious galleries on the block. The shop was an open space with only a handful of art pieces on the wall and a few abstract sculptures in the high-ceilinged room. He was sure there was longing on his face, but he couldn't stop himself from fixing his attention on each painting in turn.

People buzzed past them on their way to other destinations. Bumper-to-bumper traffic lined the street. Parking was nearly impossible, and open spaces were snapped up as people circled the streets like buzzards around fresh roadkill. Mingled with the smell of exhaust was the odor of humans mixed with various cuisine scents wafting from the outdoor cafés. Melrose was rarely quiet even during the week.

Clarke and Terri stood near the window, letting the human wave break around them.

"Man, that would be fantastic," he said after being silent for several moments.

She followed his gaze to where there was a sign that said *exhibit by Jonas Ford coming soon.*

"Yeah, it would." She stepped into him and put her arms around him, holding him close. His arm went around her in return, but he continued to peer into the gallery.

"Why not?" she asked. "Why not ask if any of these galleries would give you an exhibit? I bet one of them would take a chance on you."

Heat rose in his face, and he stepped back. Gesturing to the store, he made a small noise and turned away. Taking her hand, he pushed past the gallery and continued, then stopped.

People stepped around them, some of them making rude remarks for the two people who stood in the middle of the crowded sidewalk. A café loomed to their right, and they were blocking the entire path. She tugged on his hand to step back out of the way of foot traffic.

He pointed to the gallery they had just walked away from. "I tried. I made an appointment and went in with a portfolio and a dream. The owner did me the courtesy of scanning three of my pictures before he shut the case and slid it across his granite desk back to me. My art was too surreal, too dark, he said. They weren't commercial enough. Besides, I was who I was, and he didn't think my scandals would be good for his gallery."

Her back stiffened. "You're an addict, not the

devil. You made mistakes, but we all have. They treat you like you murdered someone."

"I did."

She furrowed her brow and pursed her lips in a silent question.

"Me. I killed me. I became just another statistic, an alcoholic in need of rehab. I made myself irrelevant in a town where all that matters is the last thing you did."

He could see her struggling with words, discarding several sentences before she appeared to find the right ones to say what she wanted.

"Start over. That's the great thing about this city. You can always start over."

"Not everyone is forgiven," he said, memories of the last two years crowding his brain.

She took his hands and gripped them. "Damn it, Clarke, stop it. Where is the man who took the world on? He's got to still be in there. These years must have been horrible for you, but they're over. You've got Kai and Harris…"

"And you, right?" His throat thickened as he asked the question. Time stopped as he waited for her answer.

"Yes. Have faith in yourself. You are good, Clarke, really good. C'mon, Kai and I didn't recognize you were the artist when we oohed and aahed over your work, remember?"

He grinned, her words giving him a hint of the confidence that had once been his hallmark. "You guys did, didn't you? I figured if you knew I had drawn the picture, you would hate it on sight, no matter what."

Her mouth twisted. "You would have been right."

"Hey, are you Clarke Masters?"

The voice was young sounding, no older than a

teenager. Clarke and Terri both turned to face the speaker.

Her age was hard to determine; she could have been anywhere from fifteen to twenty. With burgundy hair cut close to her scalp and earrings in her ears, nose, and forehead, she had a world-weary, cynical air. Tattoos laced her arms, and ink was visible on her chest and back through the light-colored crop top. Her nails were painted orange, and her fingers festooned with rings. Several long chains draped around her neck, and leather bracelets adorned her wrists.

She canted her hip at them, chewing on a piece of gum as she waited for an answer.

He grinned. The cocky smile was one he'd had a lot of practice with from his heyday. Sometimes it still made sense to go into his public persona. From the bemused expression on Terri's face, she hadn't seen one like it since she had become reacquainted with him. "Sure am. You a fan?"

"I guess." The girl said the words with a casual air of forced nonchalance. "You had some real cool tunes. I have an older brother. He turned me on to you guys. That and video games."

He fought to keep from bursting out laughing. "Video games, eh? Older brothers can be good for some things."

The crowd was still paying them no attention, eddying around the new threesome with a disgusted air.

"Hey, would you shoot me your autograph? Not that I go for that stuff, normally, but you're here and all." She tried to appear disinterested, but the woman's eyes flickered toward them.

"Clarke, why don't you sign this for her?" Terri

dug in her purse and took out one of the spec drawings they'd used for the new CD cover. Handing the image to him, she winked behind the girl's back.

"Clarke's branching into art," she explained to the girl, whose look of quick dismissal made it clear she didn't care who Terri was. "This is one of his."

She took a marker out and urged the pen into his hand.

"This is yours?" the as-yet-unnamed person asked. "It's cool."

"What's your name?" Clarke removed the cap off the pen with his teeth in a gesture he'd had years of practice to perfect.

"Jade."

He signed the card and handed the autograph to Jade.

"Hey, you should do one of those whatchamacallits," Jade said. "Where they throw your pics on the wall? Like that place down there." She pointed to the gallery close behind them.

He grinned again. "Maybe you're right. Do me a favor. Take a selfie and post to your social media. Tag me."

Jade didn't hesitate before handing her phone to Terri. "Take our picture. My brother will die of jealousy. He wanted to be Steve Jacly when he was a kid."

Terri caught his eye, and she smiled. Nothing like a teenager to remind you of your age. Or that most kids were familiar with Attraction through their older siblings or songs on interactive games.

Terri handed the camera back to Jade. The teenager opened her mouth to say something, but someone called her name. With a disgusted sigh and a roll of her eyes, Jade announced, "My mom," and hurried off.

Terri turned to Clarke. "Okay, Mr. Masters, what do you think?" She pointed to the gallery that had rejected him. "Your past can help you as well as hurt you. Those guys aren't the only game in town. There are other galleries."

A myriad of emotions surged through him, a mix of uncertainty and hope for the future.

"We'll do the legwork together. I am sure Kai will help. What do you say?"

He studied her for a long time before nodding. "Yes. I'll talk to a couple of program folks. There's all kinds of people in AA. One of them may have a lead if I put it out there. What about you, Terri?"

She blinked at his abrupt change of subject. Good. He'd intended to take her off guard.

"What about me what?"

"Your creativity. Your cooking." He gestured to a store a few doors down with gleaming stainless steel cookware in the window. "That." He turned and motioned to the Pacific Design Center visible in the distance, looming over the horizon with its large blue presence. "And that. Both of us can find our inner passion at the same time."

She made a self-deprecating gesture, slashing her hand downward. "The Pacific Design Center holds cutting edge, high-end artisans and shops, all way out of my league. You might be able to find a gallery in the huge structure that would be interested in hosting a showing, but I wouldn't find anyone who would take on an untrained chef like me. I cook, but only as a hobby. There's nothing creative about food."

"Bullshit." He was poking the bear, but damn it, he wanted her to try and follow her dream too. A shared passion would be amazing.

He could practically see her hackles rise as she bristled. Then she shook her head and shot a smoldering glance at him. "Okay, you're right," she said, pique still in her voice. "But I can't make a living at cooking. I like the stability of an office job, even though this one is collapsing around me."

He studied her, his gaze roving over her face. "Fair enough. I think you should jump off that ledge, but it's your life, not mine. Do me a favor, though, and take a class? I'll audit the course with you if that would make you happy. Indulge yourself. Do something out of your comfort zone. Follow the instructions on your notebook."

"I've checked into them…"

"Great!" He hugged her. "You'll sign up when we get home."

"I guess I won't starve."

He took note of the tremor in her voice but didn't comment. "Hey, starving artists are cool. We can be like the guys in *Rent* and just get by. Give it a shot. You have nothing to lose."

He waited to see if she would refute that statement. After a moment, Terri shook her head, and he understood that she wouldn't. Part of him wanted to press the matter, but it was her choice to make, not his.

"Speaking of starving, we came here for lunch. Let's go."

****

Later that evening Terri turned back to the computer, trying to make the results less damning with every scenario she ran. No matter what she did, she kept getting the same outcome. In desperation, she shook her mouse. All the action did was make the cells jump before settling back to rest. Nothing changed what stared her in the face in the form of an Excel spreadsheet. Numbers didn't lie.

She pulled the hair clip out of her curls and dropped it on the desk. She let out a frustrated cry before taking a deep breath and turning her attention back to the monitor. There had to be something she could do. She crunched all the numbers again, trimming to the bare essentials, trying to force a total she knew deep in her heart didn't exist.

The tuna salad sandwich she'd bought from the store on the bottom floor of their high rise petrified as she worked with the figures. Her water bottle, a reminder from Ally to drink enough liquid, also stood ignored on the desk.

She took a sip of coffee from her Apposite Records mug. The brew had long gone cold. The acrid taste burned her throat, but she swallowed anyway. She reached for the water bottle to clear her palate, then loaded the scenarios and ran through them again. Nothing changed. It stayed as bleak as it had moments before. The numbers didn't lie. Apposite had run out of time.

She raked her hand through her hair, tangling the wavy strands into hopeless snarls. She tugged at the snarls and then gave up, yanking her hand free. Her breath came out on a defeated sigh as she tried yet again. The black cursor mocked her with its slow rhythm. *Blink. Blink. Blink.*

Unless a windfall came out of Kai's meetings

today, there was no way Apposite could survive any longer.

Terri held on to that hope as she shut down the spreadsheet. All was not yet lost. If anyone could convince investors to finance Apposite, that person was Kai. She was no good at it, but her boss had a talent with people. He had done it before; he could do it again.

She picked up a medicine ball and squeezed the rubber between her fingers before dropping it again. She buried her hands in her hair and let her head fall to the desk. All those years of struggling had come down to this. Kai had tried to maintain his independence, and look where that had gotten him. If he'd sold out to another label, he wouldn't be in this position today. His label was on the verge of failing, and there was nothing she could do.

She wanted to fix things, but she didn't see any way out. Bankruptcy was the only option. That or a buyout if certain lowball offers that people had tossed out in the past were still an option. It wouldn't help her, of course, but it might give Kai something. She didn't need the help. She could find a job. This was Kai's life.

A treacherous part of her hoped if he went that route, Kai didn't, or couldn't, take her with him. Then she would be free to do what she wanted. She could cook or go back to school and get another degree. Once upon a time she'd wanted to act. If things collapsed, she could follow her dream and start living. What had begun her awakening when she met Clarke for the second time could continue.

She was still in her office, staring out the window, when Kai came back to the office. He glanced at his

Apposite watch with its lightning bolt logo.

"It's after eight," he said. "You should be home."

He unbuttoned his jacket and let his tie fall loose. Dressed in a series of olive greens, his clothes matching in tonal hues, he was every inch the professional executive. "Terri, what is wrong? Not problems with Clarke?"

"No." Her voice was flat. "Not Clarke. He's fine, I think. He left a message on my cell. I need to call him back, I guess."

"Then…what?"

She met his dark gaze, unable to read his expression. "How did your meetings go?"

He tugged on his collar, loosening the tie farther. "They went well. No promises, though."

"Possibilities?" She couldn't control the spark of hope in her tone.

He studied her for a long moment. "Nothing that will happen fast, if I understand your meaning. Is that what you are trying to say?"

She swallowed and then nodded.

He raked a hand through his hair, making the black strands stick up. "In that case, I suppose I have little option. I am going to accept Earthy Cry's offer. I checked with them, and it's still open," he said with a flat tone. "They made it clear all they will want is the catalog. The rest will be dissolved. Please keep this to yourself. You can tell Clarke, but I would prefer the rest of the office not be told until we know for sure."

She nodded. "Oh, Kai. I feel like I've failed you."

He shook his head, sorrow lining his body. "No, Terri. You did everything you could. I let you down. The failure is mine." He smoothed down his jacket with

163

an absentminded gesture. "Now go home. I am sure Clarke wants to be with you. You could use the company. Go and be with those you care about. I can handle this."

She hated to leave him, but Terri did as she was bid. Her last glimpse was of Kai standing in the doorway of his office, glancing around without recognition.

The label was ending. Her wish had come true.

Chapter Fourteen

He was waiting on the steps of her apartment when she arrived. She hadn't expected him, with her heart heavy with sorrow, but part of her thrilled at his presence.

"Hi," she said. "What's going on?"

He pulled her into his arms. "Do you trust me? If you do, I need you to give yourself to me tonight. I need you to give me everything you have and leave nothing behind. Can you do that?"

Unsure of what to expect or what had caused this, Terri nodded. She led him into the middle of her living room floor but remained silent.

He paced for a minute, his green eyes focusing like a laser on her. "Clothes off, now. I want you naked."

She shivered at his intensity.

"I need you, Terri. More than I've ever needed anyone or anything in my life. If you believe in me. If you do, take everything off."

His eyes were glittering as she did as he asked. He stood motionless, watching her movements. She removed her shirt and managed to unclasp her bra even though her hands were beginning to shake. The lacy cups joined the growing pile next to her.

Her nipples were already hard and puckered. Clarke's mouth tightened.

"So beautiful," he breathed.

She swallowed, her heart pounding, and kicked off her heels. Terri unzipped her pants and pushed the band off her waist, letting the cloth slump to a puddle around her ankles. She stepped out of them and then skimmed the purple thong off her hips and also let that drop to the ground.

"Come here." He opened his hands and gestured her forward.

She was naked, and he was still fully clothed, the bulge pressing against his jeans impressive. Fighting an attack of nerves, she went to him.

With a sudden movement, he swung her into his arms, his lips finding hers as he hauled her up. She gave him what he sought, sinking her nails into his cloth-covered shoulder as she opened her mouth to his plunder.

They had spent very little time in her one-bedroom, West Hollywood apartment, opting for his spacious townhouse or Glendale home instead. She pointed down the only hallway to the open door at the end. He carried her down the short passage with the carved moldings over the doorways. Not stopping at the threshold, he laid her down on the bed.

"Thanks, babe." He brushed a kiss across her forehead. His voice was hushed, almost reverent. "Don't close your eyes."

She complied, meeting his green gaze before he lowered his eyes, his breath catching on a gasp at her naked body.

"Yeah, like that. Keep your eyes open. Please."

He bent down and suckled one of her aching nipples, drawing the peak into his mouth and lashing his tongue over the hard bud. He repeated the action on the other nipple, and Terri moaned. She took his head in her hand and clutched at him, her hips writhing as sensation bolted through her, making her skin hot. He made a low murmur in his throat that might have been approval. His hair fell over her chest and further inflamed her senses.

"I want to be all you feel, all you see."

She was already so hot for him she could barely contain herself. All she could do was nod and relax against the pillows. Her cotton sheets were cool under her body, in counterpart to the heat pouring off him.

"You are everything." The words were as close as she could come to expressing her emotions. Her mind was spinning with feeling, the world narrowed down to just the two of them.

"Good. Very good." Still clothed, he fitted his body to hers. Plunging his hands in her hair, he kissed her with a fierce passion. She couldn't do anything but respond, the crisp hairs through the open neck of his shirt an erotic pulse against her breasts. She moaned deep in the back of her throat and rubbed her naked body over the hard ridge of his arousal.

He jerked, and his chest heaved with a sudden gasp. "You're so damned sexy," he groaned, raining kisses over her face.

She continued to move against him. Her answering spark was in the lurch of his erection against her.

"There's never been anyone like you." He marked the spaces in between her ribs with licks of his tongue. At the same time, he ran the backs of his hands down her arms, leaving goose bumps and heated flesh in his wake.

"Clarke," she breathed.

"I love the way you say my name," he growled.

He touched her nipple with his tongue in a circling motion until all she could feel was the pressure against her hard, rosy bud, sweeping around and around, sending flames shooting through her. She wanted to yank him off her breasts and thrust his head down to where she was aching and needy for him, but she also didn't want to rush things. This was a moment ripped out of time, and she wanted to savor all of it.

He moved down, and she breathed a sigh of relief, not sure how much longer she could have taken the sweet torment. Now he would bring her release.

But he seemed to be in no hurry. He kissed down the center of her torso and delved his tongue into her navel as his hands palpated her slightly rounded belly. He urged her legs farther open with his hands until they dropped wide, exposing everything to him.

She gasped when his fingers tested her readiness, tracing her moistness. Terri watched him through half-lidded eyes as he considered the close-cropped curls in fascination. Then he bent his head and again with the tip of his tongue traced her lips until she wanted to scream. He licked up and down, delving inside to taste her, but never touching her hard bud. She was screaming for him, her need so great she was drenched in sweat.

"Clarke, please," she cried, grabbing the bedframe.

"Shhh." He touched her with his thumb then, a light touch that had her arching against the digit.

She nearly wept when he left her aroused flesh and, with nips of his teeth, bit the inside of her thighs all the way down to her calves and to the top of her feet. Then he moved back up again and traced the red marks of his bites with his tongue, up and down again, leaving her shuddering.

"Oh God." The slightest touch tingled her senses. The rush of air from her ceiling fan that lifted her body hair was sensual. The brush of his blue cotton shirt against her knees made her want to weep.

"Waiting is half the fun." He kissed the front of her legs, moving back up her body.

"I…" she stammered out.

He laughed and traced her with his tongue again. Terri yelped and jumped. Everything in her wanted to grab him and force him inside her, but she would be ruining everything he was trying to prove to both of them.

He circled her, never going hard or fast enough for her to reach her peak. She moaned, thrashing her head.

"So gorgeous." He slipped two fingers inside her and stroked. She thrust against him, beyond reason, wanting what only he could give her. She would have been embarrassed if the man had been anyone but Clarke staring at her in admiration.

"Yeah, babe," he murmured and bent to her to suckle in earnest.

She was so ready she exploded the instant he gripped her with his teeth and ran his tongue over her. She cried out on a sob. He caught her hips, stilling her as he rode out the orgasm that was tearing her into small pieces and reassembling her. Pleasure washed through her with fierce intensity. She might never come back to earth.

Before she could catch her breath, he was caressing her again, and she flew apart from one second to the next, once again propelled into an ecstasy unlike anything she'd ever known.

After her third orgasm he rose and began to strip. She moved to help him, but he waggled his finger at her.

"Do you want me?" he asked when he was naked.

"Yes," she breathed, "so much."

"Tell me. Tell me where."

She was past caring about propriety. "I want you inside me. I want you to make us one person. I want only you."

His eyes darkened. As he had removed his pants, he had slipped a condom out of the back pocket. "Right answer, babe." Rolling the protection onto his erect flesh, he moved to the bed and knelt. Her mattress gave under his weight, and Terri sank down. "Because I want you too. Just you."

He urged her legs wide and pressed his tip to her opening. She bit down on her lip to suppress a long moan but couldn't resist whimpering. She thrust up, trying to draw him into her. Growling, he thrust down at the same time until he was buried all the way inside her. She cried out with relief at the feel of him.

He was shuddering, his breath coming in short pants. "I want to hold back, but oh…" His arms went rigid and his mouth worked. His eyes lost focus as he fought his body in an effort to delay his orgasm.

"No, Clarke," she whispered. "Don't think. You wanted me to give myself to you. Now give yourself to me. Lose yourself inside me."

As though the words broke his resolve, he gathered her to him as he thrust wildly, shaking in earnest. He let out a hoarse cry and then went stiff, his body pulsing.

She put her arms around him and held him close.

He collapsed, resting his head in the space where her head and neck met.

This time was different. His actions were a promise, something bigger than sex.

Terri kissed his head and moved against him. His gasp, muffled against her skin, told her of his continued arousal.

"Clarke," she said in amazement.

"Not bad for an old man, eh?" He drew circles on her nipple, which started to pucker again under his touch.

Her body tightened, and she was still excited, even after three mind-shattering orgasms. "You're ready? But you just came."

He licked the spot where her pulse beat and pressed a kiss there. "One time didn't satisfy me. I want you again. Now. Do you want me?"

"Yes."

He leaned over her, his arms supporting his weight, and began a slow movement. He thrust all the way until their bodies met, and then pulled out until just the tip of him was inside. Tension curled inside her, and it wasn't going to take much to send her over the top. She cried out as he thrust to the hilt again. At this rate she was going to climax very soon.

"Clarke, are you close? Can we come together?"

"Ohhh yeah, almost there. Tell me when."

Within two thrusts the pinnacle rushed toward her. Crying out his name, Terri dug her nails into his back, and he thrust again, throwing his head back as her contractions began.

Then they were falling together, their mutual cries of passion mingling in the air.

****

Clarke stood in the kitchen decorated in yellow and pinks, holding a pan and gazing at the stove. The older appliance had seen better days, and he wondered if the pilot light worked or if that was what the matches next to the stove were for. He stared at the pan, trying to figure out why it had been a good idea to cook for Terri. She was the chef, not him.

The phone rang. He glanced at the bathroom, then at the Caller ID. By the Maine exchange and the last name August, he had an idea who the caller was.

"Landline's ringing, babe," he called, hoping he was loud enough to be heard over the shower. "I think it's your folks."

"Crap. Answer the phone. It might be important. I'll be out in a minute."

Despite his trepidation, Clarke went to the landline and picked up the phone. "Hello?"

There was silence on the other end, a sound like wind rushed through the lines.

"I'm sorry," a woman with a sharp New England twang said. "I must have the wrong number."

"You've got the right one." Clarke mouthed a silent curse. This had been a mistake. "You're calling for Terri? Is this her mother?" This wasn't how he'd imagined meeting her colorful family. Now he wasn't quite sure how he'd pictured it. A trip back East perhaps, meeting along the rugged Maine coastline in the summertime or...now he didn't know.

"Yes." The woman's voice grew stronger. "Who are you?"

"My name is Clarke."

An intake of breath on the other side of the call

made his heart sink.

"Clarke who?"

"Masters." He said his last name without intonation, poised for whatever was coming next. This was her mother—she had to be aware of parts of Terri's history, if not all of it.

The silence on the other end was so profound that for a minute he thought the woman had hung up. Only the sound of breathing told him the line was still connected.

"I'm shocked."

He should never have picked up the phone, no matter what Terri had said. "I imagine so. Terri will be right out. Hold on." He moved to put the phone down, but her mother spoke again.

"No, wait."

Reluctantly, he did.

"I need information. Terri has told me nothing. Are you dating?"

"I'm her boyfriend."

Terri emerged from the bathroom as he said those words. Her hair was wrapped in a towel and nothing but a T-shirt clung to her body. She grinned at his words.

When he saw her reaction, his shoulders went down a few inches. "Mrs. August," he began.

"Rowenna."

"Rowenna. Terri told you what happened before?"

"Yes." Her tone was flat, but he couldn't mistake the disapproval in it. "That was a difficult time for all of us. This is quite a surprise."

"I won't hurt her this time, Rowenna." He grasped Terri's hand and tugged her to him. She went, pressing her body against his before gesturing for the phone.

Claire Davon

"You had better not. She's my only daughter, and she has been through quite enough where you are concerned."

"That's old news. This is a new beginning."

"If you say so." She paused. "Put her on."

As he handed the phone to her, he grimaced. Terri caressed his side before gripping the receiver. At least her mother hadn't hung up on him or told him off. He would take it as it came, one day at a time. He could start to build bridges there, show her family what Terri meant to him. The loneliness that had been a part of him for so many years fell away, replaced by a sense of well-being.

For the first time in a long time, he had somewhere he belonged.

****

The lined paper had names and phone numbers all the way to the bottom line and beyond, with an arrow indicating more information on the other side. Half the items had been crossed out.

"Yes, Mr. Robinson, that's him." She tried to answer the leading question from the voice on the other end with a calm she didn't feel. "No, he's not using. He's clean."

Terri shredded a piece of paper as she talked, turning the note into confetti.

"If I could just send you a few samples…" The gallery owner cut her off again, this time with a curt swear word.

"Very well, Mr. Robinson. Thank you for your time."

After hanging up, she crossed the gallery owner's name off the list with dark, angry strokes until paper

174

tore, obliterating the name.

She knew this wouldn't be easy. Art dealers were elusive, and Clarke's reputation didn't help. She had tried many angles but so far failed.

She reached for the phone again but was interrupted by a knock.

"Hello," Kai said. "Am I breaking your concentration, or can I steal you a minute?"

His manner and clothing were usually crisp, and the sight of wrinkles on his black shirt threw her. His hair was pulled back, but a few strands escaped the hair tie.

She flushed. "You caught me on personal calls." She gestured to the lined paper. "I'm trying to convince galleries to look at Clarke's work, but nobody will give him a chance."

He studied her with one raised eyebrow, a gesture she was unable to interpret.

She frowned, the action turning her lips down. "Sorry, Kai. I should be working."

He waved her sentence off with a flip of his hand. "Nothing to do right now while we iron out the details of the buyout. You have done enough for this label. Let me lend a hand. Come into my office. I want to make a call."

Kai ushered her into his space. Terri stood by the desk, watching him as he scrolled through his smartphone.

"Whatcha doing?" She wanted to clap her hands together. She put them behind her so he couldn't make out her nervous gesture.

He held up a finger and hit the speaker button. Pressing a 323 number, he motioned for her to close the door.

"Stainer Galleries," a cool female voice said.

"Fancy, hello, it's Kai Halara. I was hoping that Ricki was available to take my call."

"Hi, Kai," the woman practically purred.

Terri glanced at him in surprise. He leaned back in his leather executive chair.

"How is my favorite label owner?"

"I'm doing very well, thank you, Fancy. Are you still as beautiful as ever?"

"That wouldn't be much of a challenge if I answered the question, dear man. You'll have to come visit us and find out," the woman said in a sultry tone.

"I will do that," he agreed. "Soon."

"Wonderful. Let me put you through to Ricki."

He put his headset on and took the phone off speaker.

Ricki. Stainer. Ricki Stainer. The name rang a bell. Ricki had been a former club manager and personality at the same time Clarke was popular. Ricki had faded from the public eye, and Terri dismissed him from her mind along with everything else from that time.

"Ricki." Kai's voice was his rich, warm tone he used when schmoozing people. He turned to Terri as he spoke. "Yes, I'm doing well, thank you. Yourself? A band? One moment."

Leaning forward, he began accessing something on his computer as she waited. "Their video has gone viral online. Impressive number of hits. Thanks for thinking of me." He listened, nodding and continuing to type. "Two weeks ago I would have jumped at the chance, but there is little point now. How about if I turn your suggestion over to Plausive? I think they would do right by the band." He listened again. "I will pave the way, Ricki. That is a given. I wonder if you have a minute."

He manipulated some buttons on his computer and pressed enter. "Are you near your computer? I just sent you something I think you will find of interest." He waited, threading his index finger through the spiral phone cord. She could hear excited chatter on the other end.

"Ricki, you're going to need to trust me." Kai listened to the babble again. "This may come as a surprise when I tell you the artist's name, but have I ever steered you wrong?"

He winked at Terri, who clamped her hands around the lip of the desk, staring at him.

"It's Clarke Masters."

The chatter on the other end of the line stopped. Her heart fell.

"Ricki, I know what happened. But those pictures are amazing, and both of us know it. Imagine them on canvas hanging in your gallery. Would they not be the perfect counterpart to the fantasy art exhibit you have on display?"

The chatter started up again. Kai was silent and then motioned her over.

"Ricki, I'm going to have you talk to my vice president. She has seen the bulk of Clarke's work while I've only had the pleasure of these few paintings. If anyone can tell you the value of a Clarke Masters showing, it's Terri." He squeezed her hand as he gave her the cell phone.

She swallowed hard and then slid the phone to her ear. "Hi, Ricki." She cursed the shake in her voice. "I liked your club, the Barn, when you ran it. Fun place."

"Thanks. Did we hang out?" A hint of New York intonation was in his voice.

For a brief time, his club had been her go-to place after she was banned from the Whammy Bar, before she gave the lifestyle up.

"Nah. I wasn't around long. Anyway, about Clarke…"

"Clarke Masters. The guy was a train wreck. I bet he still is. What was your name?"

"Terri. Terri August. The collection is remarkable—that's when you really understand what he's achieved. It's so alive, so vivid. His visions come to life on canvas."

"C'mon, be real. Clarke's an addict, and they don't change. His talent doesn't matter as much as his rep. Is he going to go on some all-night bender and forget he has an exhibit the next day? I would be chancing a lot."

She clung to the faint hope that he hadn't refused outright. "I could send you pictures of his other work." She hoped her desperate edge didn't show. "Or you could come to his townhouse. Clarke is good, Ricki, and he's clean. Two years sober. Please. Just take a look and then make up your mind. I promise you won't regret giving him a shot."

There was a long silence on the other end, so long that she was sure Ricki was going to say no.

"Plenty of dudes drop out of AA with more time than he has. Two years is nice, but compared to some, it's not very long. If I say okay, does he have enough for a showing?"

She breathed a sigh of relief. "There's enough to fill several studios. His spare room in the back is stacked with paintings of all shapes and sizes."

"Can you get me shots right away? I have an unexpected opening to fill. Kai's call came at the perfect time. No guarantees, but his stuff interests me."

"Is today too soon? We can take pictures tonight and email them to you."

Kai was motioning for her to hand him the phone. "I am giving Terri and Clarke the rest of the afternoon off to give you what you need. You will have them soon." He glanced at her. "Is that enough time?"

She nodded.

"Great. We should go for drinks soon, Ricki. I am intrigued by this band you mentioned."

He signed off, and she stared at him.

"Roll up your sleeves," she said.

"What?"

"Roll up your sleeves, or take off your jacket."

His eyebrows drew together. "I'm not following your train of thought."

She grinned. "I wanted to check for rabbits or cards or anything else you might be hiding up there. You know a gallery owner? And it's Ricki Stainer? What else aren't you telling me?"

He smiled. "If one of you had told me Clarke was interested in a showing, I would have called Ricki a long time ago. We often exchange favors." He studied her again. "Clarke is serious about his painting, then."

"Very."

"He should have come to me earlier. I would have helped him."

"You know Clarke. He thinks you've done plenty already."

He nodded. "Of course. I meant what I said. Take the rest of the day off. Go photograph his paintings so he can pursue his dream. While we are on the topic of dreams, you should try for yours as well. This isn't what you want to do with your life. I can't give you much severance, but I imagine you have savings. Live your dream, Tyris August. Go to cooking school. Become the chef you were meant to be."

Fear and elation lanced through her body. The big label would absorb the Apposite catalog into their existing one. She wouldn't be in trouble when the company was sold, she'd been much too frugal for that, but she couldn't be out of work for long. Taking their position would be smart. Did cooking schools have financial aid programs for thirty-year-olds? Her notebook mocked her with its saying. *Life begins at the end of your comfort zone.*

"I don't know, Kai," she said. "Cooking is a risk."

He raised one eyebrow but made no further comment.

****

Terri glanced at the tarp-covered painting again. Clarke knew she was consumed with curiosity about what he had painted. He still wasn't ready to show her. He kept his studio locked when he wasn't there so she wouldn't sneak in to glimpse what was underneath.

He wondered what her reaction would be when he did reveal the work. He hoped she would like what he had done. The painting expressed everything that was in his soul, but he still wasn't sure how she would react. She was a tough one to read. Even though they were together, he had no idea what was going on behind her eyes. She was still self-contained, a woman who kept her emotions buried. He wondered what it would have been like if they'd been able to be together when she was still free with herself, before he had taken her spirit from her. Of all the things he regretted the most, that one topped the list.

He was in love with her. So deep in love that this was it for him. This was the great love of his life. He had read about it and even joked in the past that he had a great love—booze—but he had never expected it to happen to him. Yet here he was.

It scared the crap out of him. Sometimes he wanted to run, to get in his car and take off into the night. He had times when driving until he hit the Atlantic Ocean was a viable option. Emotion this powerful had no place in the prior Clarke's life. Wasn't that what he'd been anesthetizing himself over? Feelings? He'd done such a good job that he assumed himself incapable of this sort of emotion. Until Terri. Part of him wanted to run. The larger part of him wanted to stay and build a life.

She was positioning one of his bigger paintings to take advantage of the natural sun filling the room. She adjusted it several times, a fraction here and there, each time checking to make sure the painting was where she wanted it. She backed up and studied it and then, satisfied, lifted the camera. Staring at the frame, she fiddled with the lens. She once again checked the sight lines through the camera and then adjusted the zoom.

Light fell through the open windows and landed on her hair, turning it molten gold mixed with red fire. One beam played across the side of her face, while the other was still in shadow. The blond hair on her arm glinted in the rays. He wanted to bend over and lick each individual hair, wetting her arm with his tongue until her skin erupted in goose bumps and she melted against him. Clarke lifted his own camera.

"Terri."

She turned and he snapped a shot, ignoring her protest. She lifted a hand to ward off additional pictures.

"Don't. I'm not camera ready." She peered at him through her fingers, and he lowered the camera. He would use that shot later to paint another image of her, matching the one in his mind.

"You're beautiful." Maybe someday she would believe it.

She opened her mouth. He could see the denial forming on her lips, but then she gave him a half-grin that was so vulnerable his heart stuttered. He wanted to tell her right then and there how desperately head over heels he was for her, but the words caught in his throat.

Love. That particular emotion had never figured into his life. He had too many women and not enough time. They came in an endless, faceless stream. His lifestyle had been designed to keep people at a distance. Only in rehab had he recognized what he'd been doing. Only then had he made amends, but his reputation had done its work. Since rehab, he had resigned himself to loneliness and hunger.

There was still hunger, but no loneliness. The desperate, awful feelings had left him when Terri came into his life. She filled a hole he hadn't admitted was there.

She took the same painting and moved it in front of a drop cloth he'd set up for staging. Once again she fussed with the painting while he watched. In time he was sure that her attention to detail could get annoying, but at the moment he found it endearing.

"Any more playing with it, and I'm going to get jealous." Her sideways slanted look and her shy grin made his breath catch. He was still getting used to the understanding that he could love someone. When he had Terri in his arms, the idea wasn't so strange.

"That's something, you jealous of a painting. I'm just trying to make sure we have all the selections we need. You want choices, right, Clarke?" She held the camera away from her body. "I suck at taking pictures, but if I snap enough of them, some have to turn out good."

He didn't want options. He wanted to brand her with his body so she would always be his. He didn't want her to have anywhere to go but him. Once again he wanted to speak the emotions in his heart, but fear held him back.

"Choices are good."

Chapter Fifteen

Clarke got up from his desk. As Terri watched, he closed and locked his office door. Waggling his eyebrows, he went to her and slid his arms around her.

"Clarke," she protested. "All of them will know what we're doing." She was pressed between wood and the hard length of him against her hip.

"They're not going to, babe," he said with a wink. "We have closed-door meetings all the time. Come. Sit on my lap, and let's make out for a while."

He tugged them behind his desk to his leather executive chair. Sitting down heavily, his legs splayed, he pushed his jacket open, revealing a stark white shirt and a patch of hair under the undone buttons.

She settled herself on his lap, facing him. Their groins were touching, only the barrier of their clothes separating them.

"Good thing this chair has retractable arms." She fitted her body to his. Placing her hands on his shirt, she pushed under the cloth to his pecs below.

"Yeah. Good thing." His hands curved around her shoulders, and he urged her mouth down to his. She met his full lips, rocking against him as their tongues tangled. He groaned when she grazed his taut male nipples.

"Terri, Terri," he murmured against her lips, continuing to kiss her as he ran his hands down her spine until he covered her butt. He thrust against her, and the heat and hardness of him warmed her deep inside.

The chair creaked as their combined weights shoved it back until he was almost supine. She stretched her torso over his as he continued to thrust against her. Sun was streaming in, and she murmured a protest against his lips, gesturing to the window.

Breaking the kiss at her whimper, he turned his head. Without rising, he found the control for the blinds and brought them down, cutting off the view.

"Alone at last." His voice was harsh with need.

The noise of the chair was loud to her ears, but she knew she was imagining others could detect the squeak. Clarke and Terri were wrapped in their cocoon of desire, the outside world shoved aside.

"Clarke." His name wasn't a protest and not quite an assent as he ran trembling hands under her skirt and began to lift the cloth. He stopped and waited at the sound of her voice.

She took his hands and moved them. Then, with a deep breath, she slid the cloth up until it rode around her waist, exposing her body. She was wearing a thong, and his eyes gleamed at the sight of her bare skin.

"I like your underwear." He pressed his fingers against her and groaned, throwing his head back to the headrest.

"Do you? I thought you liked it better off."

"I do. Terri, babe…Terri," he moaned, sliding over her again and again. Without warning, he thrust a finger inside her, caressing her with his thumb.

She was about to cry out at the sudden, welcome invasion but remembered where they were and pressed her lips against his instead. He captured her tongue, thrusting in her mouth with the same rhythm as his fingers. His thumb played over her in ever tightening circles until she gasped.

She tried to pull away while sanity was still possible, but he wouldn't let her go. Without releasing her from his sensual assault, he slid the tongue down from his zipper and freed himself. He caressed her until she forgot time, space, the universe, anything but his thumb that pressed against her until she started moving against his finger in mindless need. She arched up, hands hard against his chest, and began panting. Nothing in the world matched the pleasure she was feeling now. She dug her nails into his flesh and heard the gasp of his reaction.

She was about to moan, but he covered her lips with his. Terri poured her fierce keen into his mouth as she went rigid, pleasure flooding her on a savage wave of intense release.

Replete, she opened her legs to his. He sought her out and moved inside her. She saw the need lying just under the surface when she studied his face. Slipping her arms under his suit jacket and linking them at his back, she laid her body against his and let him take the lead. Clarke held her, thrusting up inside her with uncontrolled beats of his body.

"Terri…" Moving his hands to her shoulders, he maneuvered their bodies until they were straddling each other. Then he held her against him, so close she could feel the quick beat of his heart.

Shuddering, he pressed his open mouth against her neck and suckled there. His body moved, and his nails bit into her skin as he lost control and shattered.

Even as they both began to breathe normally, she understood she had to tell him how she felt. *Soon*, she promised herself.

A knock sounded on the door. She smoothed her hands over her skirt. His face was still reddened from passion, but he grinned at her.

"Almost caught in the act," he whispered, rising with her and grazing the back of her neck with his lips. "What fun."

The Terri of a few months ago would have been embarrassed by the near miss, but all she could do was shiver at his caress.

Sun peeked in over the drawn shades, dappling them with its rays. Clarke flipped the fluorescent lights on as he yanked the door open, flooding the office with artificial light.

Kai stood there, hands in his pockets, swaying from side to side. Clarke motioned him in, glancing at Terri, who was still standing by the window.

The scent of sex probably permeated the room, but Kai looked too distracted to notice. He stepped inside, past Clarke, and closed the door behind him.

She turned to Kai with a slight frown, noting the jerky movements of his body. "Kai?" She returned Clarke's glance with a puzzled one of her own.

The click of the door lock reverberated in a room gone quiet. Kai was pale, his skin the color of copier paper.

She dabbed at a stain on the front of her skirt as Kai raked his hands through his hair. Clarke had a stain at the edge of his sports coat. Kai would have understood in a heartbeat what had gone on if he hadn't been distracted.

"What's wrong, man?" Clarke clapped Kai on the shoulder. "You look like shit."

Terri crossed the room to where the two men were standing. Her feet made little noise on the carpet, but the movement jerked Kai back into full awareness, and his eyes darkened.

"Earthy Cry Records and I have come to terms. I've sublet the office space to the bank next door. As of this morning Apposite no longer exists. I get to keep the name, but that is all." His mouth twisted. "For all the good that will do me."

Clarke slipped his hand into hers and gave her a comforting squeeze.

She returned the caress, studying him under lowered brows before turning back to her boss. Her former boss. "How long do we have?"

Kai heaved a sigh, and her heart went out to him. The label had been his dream, his vision, and now those dreams had crumbled to dust.

"Friday. Everyone is being let go—the company is being dissolved. They would like to keep Terri on as a consultant for a few months during the transition."

Clarke didn't appear surprised. Concern, compassion, and something she couldn't name were written on his face when he met her gaze.

Her love for him surged up in a wave before she turned her attention back to the issue at hand. Kai still stood in front of them, his shoulders bowed.

"Do they know?" Clarke gestured to the office outside the door.

Kai shook his head, continuing to rock back and forth on his heels. "I wanted to alert you first. It's hitting the news now, though, so we'd better tell them.

I…"

Terri put her arms around Kai and embraced him. Kai gathered her close, pressing against her like she was a lifeline.

"I'm so sorry, Kai," she whispered, feeling the cool silk of his jacket under her palms. "This was your dream."

He sighed again. "I managed to wrangle a severance for people." Releasing her, he stepped back. Emotion swirled behind his eyes and in the lines bracketing his mouth, but his face was dry. "I'm going to work for Shatter Sound Records for six months. After that, who can say?" He shrugged, the movement making the shoulders of his jacket flex.

"I don't want severance." Clarke's voice was husky. "I didn't earn the money."

Kai nodded and held out his hand to Clarke. He took the proffered hand and shook with a firm grasp.

"I'll make a note of that. I'm proud to know you." Kai sighed one final time and turned to the door. "Time to tell the others."

He appeared lost, defeated, and so alone that her heart broke.

Linking one hand with Kai and the other with Clarke, she gestured to the door. "Your trusty lieutenant wouldn't desert you in the heat of battle." This was a moment she would never forget. Standing next to the man she loved, even with her future in chaos, she was alive.

****

There was so much to do. So many files to pack up. Artwork had to be transferred, and masters had to be warehoused. All the data on their computers was downloaded to flash drives or online to transfer to Earthy Cry Records. The computers were being wiped clean and sold to the employees or a secondhand store. The furniture was being taken away. People came and went from the offices, and the days went by in a flash.

The staff was gone, but Terri and Clarke stayed to help Kai shut the office down. She had agreed to a meeting with Earthy Cry's HR department. The move was practical, like her.

After work they were too exhausted to do much more than fall into bed. She couldn't wait for things to settle down so they could talk. She didn't know how much longer she could keep her love inside.

She found Kai and Clarke in the main lobby, at the reception desk. Above their heads, a worker was removing the letters and stylized lightning bolt that had been the Apposite Records logo.

"Nothing left but office supplies." Kai kept his head turned away from the sight of the falling logo. "Take anything you need, and I'll give Earthy Cry the rest."

"Ah, man," Clarke said. "If I were still a drinking man, I'd take you out and get you trashed."

"Don't you dare." Kai met Clarke's gaze, his tone low and rumbling.

"Don't worry."

Nobody could ever be sure with an addict. He had told her that many times. But he'd come so far. Surely he wouldn't fall back into that self-destructive pattern again. He had too much to lose now.

Kai turned his head to watch the logo turn into dust and shards. "That which does not kill you makes you stronger."

"Amen." Clarke glanced at Terri as he said it.

The scrape of the putty knife seemed too loud. Bits of plaster fell with a thud to the heavy tarp below the ladder. Kai winced as they collided with the ground.

"It's still yours, Kai. They can't take your dream from you. You can try again when you get back on your feet."

His shoulders slumped. That had happened a lot in the past few days.

She shot Clarke a worried glance, and he swallowed.

"Kai, you are smart, young, and business savvy."

A dusting of grime lay over Kai's hands and body. A faint plume rose from him when she put her hand on his shoulder. He stared at her.

"This didn't work. The timing was bad. Take a deep breath, get back on your feet, and try again. If this guy…" She pointed to Clarke, and he stepped in back of her and put his hands on her shoulders. "If he can remake himself, then are you telling me a little thing like your business going under is going to defeat you? Defeat Kai Halara? I don't think so."

She met Kai's gaze with fierce intensity until a grin played over his lips.

"You're one of a kind." He touched her cheek before dropping his hand. "Thanks."

Clarke's hands tightened on her shoulders. He had tensed when Kai touched her.

Could Clarke be jealous of Kai? The notion was ridiculous, but Kai backed up a step, and Clarke breathed out in what sounded like relief. The idea that he could feel jealousy gave her hope for their future.

After the show on Saturday. That would be the

time to tell him. All the pieces of their lives would be squared away, and they would have plenty of time for love.

Chapter Sixteen

She groaned as Clarke's tenor filled the bedroom of his townhouse, belting out about beautiful mornings and days. The sun through the blinds told her the time was around nine o'clock.

"Too early for show tunes." She opened one eye to observe the still-naked man standing by the window. "Clarke, people will be able to appreciate you in all your glory if you keep standing there."

He scratched his chest and pounded it lightly like a caveman. "Never too early for *Oklahoma*. Come on, up. The equipment will be at the Rumble at eleven, and I'd like to be there for load in. The guys are all going to be there, and I want to help too."

"You want to help?" She remembered the old singer who didn't lift a finger to aid his roadies when they set up shows.

He leaped on the bed, legs bent, creating a hollow in the mattress when he landed. Then he straddled her, his hands at her waist. "I do, and I will. As for people seeing me—they can look but they can't touch," he said. He kissed her, a swipe of his lips across hers. "My body is yours and yours alone. Come on." He got up again and extended his hand. "Let's shower. Then I need food. Got a big day ahead of me, and I need my cereal."

She gave his large form a long once-over.

"Cereal?"

He grinned, his good mood spilling into the room. "Yeah, you know, cereal. It's usually made out of grain…athletes and celebrities love the taste." He tugged the covers off her naked body and hauled her to her feet. "Shower. Food. Rumble. In that order."

She let herself be led. Nothing could be better than this perfect day with this incredible man. Tonight was the night. It made for good synergy to tell him after he'd gotten back on stage. After the show she would confess her feelings and hope they were returned.

The night was too far away and rushing in on her at the same time.

The Rumble was already bustling with activity when Clarke and Terri arrived. A large gear truck was parked in the parking lot by the back door, and unfamiliar people were moving in and out of the club, loading equipment into the backstage area.

Clarke waved at Harris, who was helping with amplifiers. With a jerk of his head, Harris acknowledged the greeting and indicated that Clarke could help him. He kissed Terri and joined Harris. She watched them for a minute, admiring Clarke's muscles under his plain gray T-shirt. Steve Jacly, a slight, intense man, and his wife, Dana, were also helping. Both shook Terri's hand when Clarke introduced them. By the puzzled expression in Dana's eyes, Terri was aware that the other woman recognized her. The couple had met and married at the same time she was chasing Clarke.

Someday she might not feel the shame of her early behavior. Someday she might be able to forgive herself for not understanding the difference between lust and love. It had taken her until now to get it. Love wasn't trying to force someone into her version of who she wanted them to be; it was wanting the best for her partner. Love was wanting to wake up next to them and enjoying their company, even if the only thing they were doing was watching TV or arguing over the remote.

Love was Steve and Dana's enduring marriage. Love was seeing her man stretch his wings, face his fears, and help her tackle hers. Partnership was doing things together, watching out for each other and always being there for each other. For the first time she understood how her parents had stayed married all those years. She loved Clarke, yes, but she also liked him. Back then she hadn't liked the man who was so careless with others.

After load in, they went to the Whammy Bar. She eyed the familiar façade with its doorway, outside smoking area, and bushes with apprehension. While she doubted the owners would stop her from coming in, fear rushed through Terri as she entered. To her relief, the man seating them was a man she recognized but who did not appear to place her.

The meal was a pleasant affair, with the guys chatting about long-ago events. Steve was quiet, directing the bulk of his conversation to Dana, whose affection for her husband was clear. Occasionally he glanced at Terri, a wealth of questions in his dark eyes. He reminded her of Kai, with the same watchful, intense quality that took in everything. Steve Jacly and her had intersected, here and there, but not for very long. She wondered what he was thinking but couldn't tell. Even back then Steve had been reserved, his conversation perfunctory. How Clarke had managed to drag this man to clubs was a miracle.

Clarke had become bombastic, sallying forth about old times and holding court. The table was talking about old times, and none with more force than him.

He caught her grin and leaned over. "What's so funny, babe?" he whispered with a twinkle in his eye.

"You." She nudged his side with her shoulder. "You're expounding." She gestured to the restaurant, which was bare of patrons besides them. "It's cute."

He opened and then closed his mouth. "You mean I'm being pompous." He rubbed his hand over her leg, his grin bubbling at the corners of his lips.

"A little," she agreed. "You're adorable. I love that old confidence in you."

"I feel awesome." Then he frowned. "Still, I'll stop. I shouldn't be hogging the spotlight."

"Awesome is a good word." She kissed him on the cheek and urged him back to his storytelling. With his hand still on her thigh, he picked up the thread about their early days and continued his conversation with Harris but at a lower tone, letting the others converse amongst themselves.

****

She had gone back to his townhouse to shower and change. She promised him he would like what she wore. He told her he didn't care, but the garment bag that hung in the bedroom closet spoke of a dress short enough to keep him hard the entire evening.

Alone in the small dressing room, Clarke ignored the fruit and cheese plates and began to pace. Love was an unfamiliar emotion to him. Sure, he'd fancied himself in love about a hundred times over the past twenty years, but they had been transitory feelings, gone as quickly as they came. This was different.

He raked his hand through his hair.

One gray-eyed strawberry blonde was capable of sending him to the moon or to hell. There was no getting around it. He was in love with her. Way in love. Not the sort of love that faded next month, this was an all the way thing. This was housekeeping and vows and babies and rings and...shit.

He didn't know what was inside her head. She might be as in love with him as he was her or perhaps this was a passing thing. He sat in the makeup chair and then launched back out. His good mood earlier faded with the understanding that they were near showtime. He had been insane to agree to do this show. They broke up too many years ago, and the music scene had changed too much. Yeah, the marquee said sold out, but that likely was mostly comped industry people, half of whom wouldn't be there. So what if people were already starting to line up down the side of the Rumble, sitting on the ground while waiting for the doors to open three hours from now.

Sound check had started. He could tell by the "check, check, check, one, two" voice below him. Time to go down there.

A knock rapped on the door, and then Dana peeked around the wood. "Clarke, they need you downstairs."

She stepped into the room and shut the door behind her. They were neither friends nor enemies. She was a woman he admired for her spirit and spark as well as her looks. He had chased her before she smacked him down. Now she was his friend's wife, and he respected that commitment. He should have back then.

"Is everything okay?" she asked, a thread of concern in her voice. "Are you okay?"

"Sure. I'm fine." His lack of enthusiasm would be easy to read. "I'm just wondering why the hell I imagined this would be a good idea."

"Steve said the same thing yesterday. You guys are going to do great. Haven't you been on Attraction's page? The buzz is incredible."

"Sure, but that's social media. It's not reality. Everything I've been doing lately is to build awareness of the label. Fans can say a lot of things. That doesn't mean they're going to care when I get up there." His hands clenched into fists before he made a conscious effort to relax them. Sweat beaded along his forehead, and a muscle jumped in his jaw.

"Clarke, you're nervous." Dana's mouth dropped open.

"Yeah." He glanced at her from under lowered brows. "I haven't been on a stage in years. It's not like riding a bike. I'm a painter now, not a singer."

"You're a performer. Do what you do best. Entertain. On a random aside, Terri?"

She didn't need to say the words "little Maine stalker." Just because his memory was shot didn't mean that was true of others. "Terri," he affirmed. "Things are different now."

She nodded, her disbelief written in the slow movement. "If you say so. We all are, I suppose. You're happy?"

"I am. That scares the crap out of me."

She studied him, and a dawning awareness lit her too-observant face. "Clarke, you're in love."

"Yeah." He said the word almost to himself. "That

is what is so terrifying."

"I never thought I'd see the day, or that you would end up with her. Lynx was a nightmare at the end. Congratulations."

He lurched around the room, his attention going from object to object. "Let's get sound check over with."

She touched his arm, stilling his progress. He stopped and turned his head to meet her gaze but stayed facing forward.

"Sorry. I'm getting used to the new you. There's been a lot of time between then and now. We all have adjustments to make."

He passed his hand over his eyes and then pressed his fingers over hers. "Thanks."

"If you're a good person now, that's all anyone can ask."

He nodded, but his mouth was dry.

A man was in his dressing room when he returned from sound check. The unfamiliar man had the sweaty, wrung-out look of a longtime coke user. Clarke darted a glance back toward the open door.

"Hey, man," the guy said. "How's it shaking, brother?" He slapped at Clarke's hand, and Clarke returned the gesture. Now he recognized the man. He'd gone to some Narcotics Anonymous meetings with a court card in hand, but not lately.

"Hey, Randall." He slipped into a polite, distant tone. "Long time no see. Last time I laid eyes on you was at an NA meeting."

Randall scoffed. "Those NA crap things are for losers. I got my card filled out and bolted. Nothing wrong with blow. Matter of fact, I've got some. Want to do a line?"

He pushed aside the items on the vanity and wiped the glass off with his sleeve. Then he took a baggie and shook some granules onto the surface. It had been years since Clarke was around the white crystals, and the old craving hit him like a shockwave.

"I'm not using. I'm in the program." He eyed the drug, his mouth watering. Damn. He needed to call his sponsor. Right now.

Or did he?

Randall cut the coke into four stripes and then handed Clarke a straw. "Come on," he said with a nudge and a wink. "A few won't hurt you. Coke will get you amped for the show. Didn't you used to say you needed it to perform?"

He stared at the straw in his hand and back at the neat lines of white powder.

****

Terri entered the club with a fixed smile, whistling tunelessly. Her heart kept skipping a beat as curls of both dread and anticipation warred for dominance inside her.

"Wowza." Harris crossed the room to intercept her. "Looking good, hot stuff."

The black halter dress was simple, falling in a straight skirt to about two inches above her knee. She had on heels an inch higher than she was used to, and had had her hair and makeup professionally done. Dressing up should have helped calm her nerves, but all it did was remind her of those old days.

Harris leaned on a pole and gave her a slow perusal. "Throw Clarke over and run off to Vegas with me." The wicked leer told her he wasn't serious. "I'll make an honest woman of you."

She batted her eyelashes at him. "Who says I want to be made an honest woman of? Maybe I like the idea of living in sin. Maybe that suits me."

His eyes sparkled with admiration. "I can't believe you're the same person." He swept her into a quick hug and released her. "I didn't think I'd be alive on the day when Clarke got himself a real girlfriend."

I never thought Clarke would be with you, were the words he didn't say, but they were as clear as day.

"Life is strange. I'm amazed some days myself." She stepped away. "Have you checked out the line waiting to get in? It goes all the way down the block."

"Cool. We need it." He eyed her, and his hands flexed, but he moved away. "Clarke is upstairs."

She watched the light and sound guys check their equipment and then headed up to his dressing room.

The door was halfway open, so she pushed on it, preparing to drape herself over the doorway and flip her hair back dramatically. All thought of performing that action stilled when the scene unfolded before her. Her blood went cold, and her hand fell from the door to thud against her side.

This wasn't happening.

Clarke and a man she didn't know stood there with straws in their hands, staring at four straight lines of what had to be cocaine. She'd seen him with a straw up his nose before. But not since he'd returned to her life. Not since Clarke 2.0.

"Oh God, Clarke, tell me this isn't what it looks like."

His mouth twisted into a parody of a smile. His face set into firm lines, and she couldn't tell what he was thinking.

Deny it, please. She prayed for him to tell her it wasn't true. She would believe him. She needed him to say the words.

Clarke put the straw down on the vanity and stepped away. "I...damn, Terri, is that what you're thinking?" His face twisted, and for a moment he appeared much older than his age. "After all this?"

A shocked gasp escaped her, and her hand flew to her mouth.

The stranger bent down and snorted two lines, one into each nostril, before straightening. "Your turn." He gestured to the vanity.

Clarke didn't move, continuing to stare at Terri.

She pointed at the drug, clamping her jaw for a moment to keep from screaming. *Deny it, Clarke. Just deny it.*

When he said nothing further, she backed up a step.

"Go ahead. I guess that's what you want. I...Clarke..." Her breath left her on a choked sob. She waited again, hoping against hope he would say something, call her an idiot for doubting him, and scatter the remaining two lines into dust.

He turned away, facing toward the vanity and the guy still standing there, holding out the straw. When he spoke, his voice was bitter and cold. "Go, Terri. If that's what you think, get out of here."

She whirled and ran.

Chapter Seventeen

She had no idea how she got home that night. Once home she turned off her phones, both the landline and her cell, and tried to go to sleep. What little sleep she got was fitful and sparse, and as soon as the tendrils of daylight shone over the horizon, she got up.

Her hand shook before she turned her cell back on. Clarke hadn't left any messages, neither on her answering machine nor on email. She had two calls from Ally, wondering where she was, and one from Kai, but nothing from the man who had reminded her of how stupid she'd been to think they could escape their past. At the end of the day, he would always be an addict and her a stalker.

Terri got in her car, drove to her favorite Mulholland Drive turnout at the top of the mountain, and parked. She sat on the grass a little way down the hill and stared over the view of the San Fernando Valley. Not even the brown haze of smog that lay over the flat land took away from the beauty of the twinkling lights and city streets.

She thumbed to the official Attraction social media sites and read. She was punishing herself but was still unable to stop from checking. The fans were buzzing about the incredible show at the Rumble the night before. They said Harris and Steve had fallen into their old routine. They dueled with their guitar and bass, chasing each other around the tiny area and playing off the other one's musical talent. Harris had jumped off the stage and played to the women in the audience.

The fans posted about how great Clarke looked, about his banter, the way he interacted with the loyal following at the club. At one point he knelt down to sing to a woman in a wheelchair in front, something he would never have done in the past.

Nobody once mentioned that he appeared high or incoherent. Person after person wrote about how on pitch he was, how he commanded the fans to do his bidding. They hung on every word, per the reviewer, mesmerized by his return to the old Clarke. Several alluded to his performances in early Attraction shows before the addiction had taken hold of him.

She picked up a rock and hurled it down the steep slope. Even though the sun was rising, a chill still nipped the morning air. Terri rose to her feet and dusted the grass off her jeans, wishing she'd brought a jacket.

She remembered the bleak misery on his face when she had begged him to deny that he had relapsed. Still, he'd had the straw in his hand and a line ready. What else was she supposed to think?

She walked back to her car with heavy footsteps. She had asked him, and he didn't say he hadn't. He had taunted her with his cold words, and she had run. He was an addict and couldn't be trusted. He'd said so himself. Even though he hadn't said it, the words "little Maine stalker" reverberated under his tone. Their past would always be there between them, impossible to escape. How stupid she'd been to think either one of them could get free of who they were.

When she arrived home, she had nowhere to go

and nobody to report to. She had no spreadsheets or bank statements to balance. No covers to design or new bands to listen to. For the first time in ages, she was at loose ends.

The applications for the cooking schools were strewn across her kitchen table, filled out, and ready to send back. She could do this. She could follow her dream. That was utterly stupid. She should have known better than to try and follow her dreams. That offered nothing but heartache. She should stuff all of that in the wastebasket and forget it.

The pamphlets lay there, mocking her. Taking the job with Earthy Cry was the smart thing. She would go on that interview and accept. No dreams of cooking or of a life with Clarke.

She had poured a cup of coffee when her doorbell rang.

Her heart leaped.

"Who is it?" She checked her reflection in the toaster, both hoping and fearing it would be Clarke.

"Kai."

The hopes and doubts came crashing down to earth with a thud. "Go away, Kai. You're not my boss any longer. I'm not in the mood for a lecture."

There was a short pause. "Let me in, Terri. We need to talk. I smell coffee. You can at least give me a cup."

With a sigh, she went to the door to let him in.

His brow creased at her puffy and blotchy face. *So what*. She didn't care what her old boss—or anyone— thought.

"Shouldn't you be at the new label?" She punched the door shut, and it closed with a bang.

"Wednesday. I needed a few days to take care of some loose ends." He met her gaze with a solemn expression. "Pour me a cup?"

She reached for the mugs. The first one she pulled out was an Apposite logo giveaway she'd brought back from the office in her pile of personal property. She went to shove the cup back in the cupboard, but he stopped her.

"That is fine, Terri. That is perfect. A reminder of the good times."

He stood in her kitchen, a tall, dark presence, until she motioned him to sit. He sat straight in the chair, studying her.

"You should always remember the good times." She handed him his mug of black coffee, glad her hand wasn't shaking.

"Truer words were never spoken." He was quiet for a moment. "Terri, don't take that job at Earthy Cry. Pursue your dream." He gestured to the pamphlets.

She followed his movement and shook her head. "Why, Kai? What has pursuing my dreams ever gotten me but pain?"

He set the cup down on the table. "If you still worked for me, I would fire you. My dear former Vice President, life is a risk. Take a chance. Try cooking. Do it for a semester. If you find you can't live without the uncertainty, then I will give you a glowing reference. But try first before you say no."

She let the silence fill the room before shaking her head in an indecisive movement. "I'm not built that way."

"I think you are. One semester, Terri. Just one."

She lowered her eyes. "I'll consider it, okay?"

"Thank you." He took another sip and then raised his dark eyes to her. "I am sure you understand why I am here. Clarke went on stage and sang without any indication his heart was breaking. He gave the audience the performance of a lifetime, leaving them cheering for an Attraction reunion. Why, Terri?"

She took a sip of the coffee, staring into the cup instead of at her former boss. When she met his gaze, it held curiosity and incomprehension but no condemnation.

"What did Clarke say?"

"Nothing. Harris asked him, but he refused to answer. You should have been there. He lived up to his billing. He was larger than life, a true front man."

Her throat clogged, and she once again found she couldn't speak.

"Tell me why. Clarke was shattered, and I want to understand what you did to my friend."

She whirled on him, all the bottled-up emotions surging to the forefront in a blinding rage. "What *I* did to *your* friend?" she blurted out. "Didn't *your* friend tell you about the dealer that was there that night? Didn't *your* friend tell you he was there with Clarke, alone in a dressing room with several lines on the table and straws in both of their hands? Did *your* friend bother to tell you he was using again?"

Kai had gone impassive again. Folding his hands over his chest, he studied Terri as she erupted, saying nothing.

"Yeah, that's right. I caught *your* friend in a dressing room with some swine of a dealer, straw ready and poised over lines of coke. It had to be good stuff, not that I have any experience with that sort of thing. I hope he enjoyed his blow."

His eyes were dark and unreadable. She gulped down another large mouthful of coffee and choked, coughing on the too-quick swallow. Anger, clean and pure, cut through her, an emotion she was unable to take out on the real target of her misery.

"Are you finished?" he asked.

She jutted her chin in the air. "For now."

"Good. Did you witness Clarke doing the lines?"

She shook her head. "No, but…"

"Did he say he had been doing them?"

She traced the memory in her mind, not that the images had left her for one second. "No, but…"

"Did the dealer say they'd been doing them?"

"Kai, you don't understand!"

"Enlighten me. You two have something special. Tell me why you're throwing your relationship away."

She looked at her former boss, a man with problems of his own. Her anger deflated. "You want to know why? I asked him, and he didn't deny it. He had that straw in his hand and said nothing." She tapped her head.

"I see."

He remained silent for so long, his dark eyes focused down on his coffee cup, that she broke.

"See what?" Rage made her tone sharp. "What are you trying to tell me, oh so wise Kai Halara?"

When his dark gaze met hers, she tried not to flinch at his sorrow. His eyes held misery, deep and haunting, telling a wordless tale of a broken past. "In my world, Terri, love means trust. Love means believing in someone unconditionally. I have never found the kind of affection that the two of you share, but put yourself in Clarke's position."

She frowned. "What do you mean?"

"You know what Clarke has been through in the past few years. Even his family doesn't think he can stay clean. Then the one person in the world who is supposed to believe in him, the woman he loves…"

"He's never said he loves me."

"Hasn't he? Maybe he has not said the words, but every action, every touch of his hand tells me he does. Examine his deeds and tell me that isn't love."

She opened her mouth and then closed it, a collage of images going through her mind. Clarke losing control the first time he touched her. Clarke in the diner, so sure she would leave him because of his past. Clarke at the office. Clarke at Mulholland, picking a wild purple flower and tucking the bloom behind her ear. Clarke on that incredible night. *Clarke*.

"I've known Clarke for five years, from when he was still using to today. He struggles with his addiction every day, but he faces it down. You should have made him stronger, not weaker."

Her eyes filled with tears. The truth of ten years ago beat on her, and she opened her mouth, but nothing came out. He studied her for long moments.

"I…" The words were so hard. Saying what she wanted to meant telling her boss her ugly secrets, the things that made her fallible.

"Terri, while you and I have been colleagues for the same length of time, I don't understand what makes you tick. You've always had a wall around you that nobody could penetrate. I'm your friend; you can trust me. Nothing you can tell me would make me think less of you."

His final words were her undoing. She sat down heavily in a kitchen chair and blurted out the whole story to Kai. She left nothing out, not her absurd behavior, not Clarke's reaction, not the way people abandoned her.

When she finished, she was breathing hard, her chest heaving with effort. Tears threatened, but she took several breaths and averted her face to blink them away.

His face was a mask, his expression impossible to discern. "Clarke was a real asshole back in the day."

She blinked, the unexpected words making her mouth fall open. "I was the one who chased him…" she began, but he continued on as though she hadn't spoken.

"He is aware this girl, barely a woman, practically still a teenager, has a crush on him, and he does little to prevent it. She keeps throwing herself at him, and he allows it, doesn't truly discourage it, and then one night when he is bored and horny, he sleeps with her, only to tell her to get better material and try again. That's a jerk move all around."

"I stalked him. I am to blame."

He set the mug down and beckoned her to him. When she went, he tugged her into his arms and hugged her. She was stiff for a moment and then relaxed against him, the tears that had threatened moments before slipping free and sliding down her cheeks.

"You were a child. You behaved inappropriately, but he was the adult, and he should have done better."

His words were muffled against her ears, but each one slid home.

"That's the same thing my mother said. Before I stopped telling people stuff, I told Mom everything. She said pretty much what you just did."

He pushed back a little and brushed a tear away from her cheek. "Poor Terri. You've kept the real you hidden all these years, thinking people would judge you. But nobody could be as harsh on yourself as you have been. Thank you for telling me. Thank you for trusting me with the real Terri. I like her. I think I would have liked you ten years ago. Wild, impulsive, fearless. That woman is still inside you. Let her out." He cupped her chin. "I'm sorry my friend was an asshole."

That got a startled beam from her, which she suspected was his intent.

"I've spent a long time hating myself for those days. It's going to take me a while to believe in myself again. I love him, Kai. How do we get past this?"

His eyes were dark, compassion gleaming through their depths. "Neither of you are the people you were. You are who you are, and that is all that matters."

"Who is that person?" She was near tears and biting her lip. It quivered against her teeth despite her efforts.

"Ah," he said. "So many people. You are a wonderful, unique woman, and your flaws make you human. You are my friend, and I love you. I love Clarke as well, but he was a bastard." Kissing her forehead, he brushed her hair back.

All she could do was stare at him, but she couldn't read his eyes.

Her landline rang, the jangle loud in the still room.

"I suspect you will want to answer that." Kai stepped away from her and toward the door. "I can let myself out."

She crossed the room and snatched up the phone, trying to control her slamming pulse. The Caller ID confirmed her suspicions—and her hopes. "Clarke?" Despite her best efforts, her voice was trembling.

"Terri." His tone was raw and husky. "Would you come over? I'd love to talk to you if you're willing."

Chapter Eighteen

Terri raised her hand to knock on Clarke's door and then lowered it. Taking a deep breath, she tried again. Once again her courage failed her. Desolation had been in his eyes when she flung her accusation at him, a furious pain that even now haunted her dreams.

Raising her hand before she could fail again, she knocked, three loud raps he should be able to hear even from the seclusion of his workroom.

She waited. The rear fender of his car confirmed that he was home, but when he didn't answer immediately, her worst fears clawed to the surface. Maybe he had changed his mind, even though he called less than an hour ago. Maybe he had left and didn't want to face her.

The soft tread of bare feet stopped in front of the peephole to the outside. Trying not to appear nervous, she fixed her attention on the hanging plant to the left of the door where a hardy pothos hung. Despite inconsistent watering and a less-than-ideal spot, the plant thrived.

Clarke opened the door. Backlit against his hall light, his hands shoved in the pockets of his pants, he had a five o'clock shadow and uncombed hair. His baggy sweats and a sleeveless, gray Attraction T-shirt that was stained with paint appeared to be slept in. The living room smelled of oils mixed with resin, and she wondered if he'd spent the past hours doing nothing but painting.

"Hi," she said, twisting her hands around each other. In answer he widened the door and stepped back, not so much inviting her in as letting her. She stepped inside, and he shut the door behind her. Then he leaned against the doorway and crossed his arms, his face unreadable.

She tried to speak, and nothing came to mind. There was no good way to frame the words to ask the question that had been lurking in her mind since the show. Detritus of his night's activities was evident throughout the townhouse in the sketches strewn on many surfaces.

"Thank you for coming."

She heard huskiness in his voice, and so much pain was in his eyes. Terri bit her lip and focused her attention to the floor.

"I…" He trailed off, paused, and cleared his throat. "Damn, this is tough."

She moved past him and picked up a sketch sitting on the floor, depositing it on the coffee table before even being aware she had done so. "Why, er, why did you call me?" she finally managed to get out, not meeting his gaze.

He uncoiled at that with a rapidity that made her blink. He strode to the doorway and paused there, his back to her. Then he turned around. Such hurt was in his face that she blinked again.

"I owe you an apology, Terri." He stopped again. Tension radiated through the stiff lines of his normally fluid body.

She wanted to reach out a hand to him but stopped

herself.

"I am so sorry. You have no idea how sorry." His Adam's apple worked as he swallowed.

The breath went out of her at the sorrow etched in his body. His gaze bounced off hers, settling for a spot beyond her.

He was apologizing. That was what he was supposed to do as a member of AA, right? Step nine and direct amends. That was what he was doing. Making amends. This was what people did in twelve-step programs.

When she stayed quiet, he gave her a hooded stare. "When you questioned me, I went blank. I should have just denied it, but I left you room to doubt. And given my history, you had every reason to be wary."

Tears pricked her eyes. Ninth step amends. She was pretty sure that was the step. That was why she was here. He was doing his part, per the values of his program. That might be all this meant.

"Thanks, Clarke. Apology accepted. I am sorry too. I shouldn't have accused you of using drugs." She crossed her arms, suppressing the desire to go and kiss the hurt out of him. Too much had been said too recently, and she couldn't bring herself to risk it. Instead she dug her nails into the skin of her biceps.

Grief lined his face, and his eyes grew moist. "Do you think I did?" he asked, desolation in every line of his body.

Kai's words came to her, and she turned them over in her mind. Not until he straightened and sighed did she understand he was still waiting for her answer.

"No. I don't think you did. I don't think you would let your addiction take you down that easily. Not you.

Not the Clarke Masters I know." *Not the Clarke Masters I love.*

He breathed out, exhaling a sigh. "Thank you. That means the world to me."

"You're welcome."

"I had that straw in my hand and the lines in front of me, and I was tempted. I can't lie about that. But I didn't. I didn't," he repeated. "I threw Randy out and called my sponsor. I've upped my meetings. I've been dry, but I was near relapse. Sometimes you can only see it after the fact. I've got a lot to work on. I can't hold the past against people when I've got so much baggage of my own. Today is all that matters. Thank you for accepting my apology."

She let out a breath of relief and anguish. "Clarke, all this." Her voice was shaking, matching the trembling in her body. "Is this just an amends? Something you have to do for your program?"

He stared at her for a moment. Then he gestured with his head to the hallway that led to his workroom. "C'mon. I want to show you something."

She followed him to his workroom. The mingled odors were much stronger here, as she had gotten used to. The light was muted, the windows still covered by heavy drapes to block the sunlight. Paintings were stacked against every wall of the otherwise bare room with the ones selected for the gallery showing in one corner.

The covered picture rested on the support in the middle of the room. Terri's gaze flicked to it. The piece was the only one he hadn't let her photograph, despite everything.

"I didn't want to show you this until I was happy

with it." His big body blocked the easel as he lifted the tarp up. He took the object off the stand, handed the painting to her, and stepped away.

She stared at the painting, the impact of it not hitting her immediately.

The image was of her face, so alive and full of emotion it glowed with internal light. Her eyes were blazing with passion, something he must have seen in her in the aftermath of their lovemaking and translated to canvas. He'd captured the myriad colors of her hair, interweaving red and blond and ash until each strand danced with individual fire. But what caught her most was the softened promise in her parted lips and sleepy eyes. The images told her that Clarke had been feeling the same breadth of emotions she had.

She studied the painting for a long time, afraid to touch the canvas in case the paint was still wet, and then up at him. She couldn't hide the emotions she was feeling, not this time. Her lips were trembling, and her eyes were full of tears. Truth bubbled inside her, taking her breath away.

"Oh, Clarke. You did love me after all. You loved me."

His head dipped, and he folded his hands across his chest. "Yeah. I loved the crap out of you. If love means wanting that person with you every second of the day. If love means waking up and putting my hand out to make sure you're still there. If love means picturing you round with my children. I can't say if that's the way that it's supposed to be, but I sure as hell loved you. I'm sorry I did what I did. After our past, that was unforgiveable."

She put the painting back on the easel, unable to

control the trembling of her hands. They started shaking in earnest as the tears overflowed and escaped from her eyes, rolling down her cheeks as she battled her emotions.

Loved. Every sentence had been in the past tense. He had *loved* her. Not love present tense, loved past tense. They might have apologized and forgiven each other, but that didn't mean the emotions were the same. Some things left too big a mark to overcome.

Gripping the edges of the easel, Terri's shoulders shuddered as she surrendered to the desolation inside and began to sob. Small cries escaped her at the knowledge of what had happened. She had lost the only man she'd ever loved. Clarke Masters. They'd met at the wrong time and wrong place. They had carried their baggage around like weapons. They had been two messed up people who grew into adults that found their way to each other. They had hurt each other and made mistakes, and through all that there had been love. She should have told him ages ago. She'd waited too long.

Fat tears rolled down her face, and her voice came out in choking sobs. "You loved me, oh God. Loved me." She could barely get the words out.

His presence loomed behind her before his hands closed on her shoulders. His hands were trembling as he pulled her close. "Terri, you're crying. Oh, babe. I've never seen you cry. You're always so controlled." He rocked her against his body. "Shh, shh. Don't cry. I still do," he whispered, his arms closing around her and locking at her belly. "Oh, Terri, love. Please don't cry. I'm torn up inside." He dropped a kiss against her shoulder and rested his head against hers as he continued to hold her close, swaying with her. "I love you, Terri. Please."

"You do?" She twisted around. "After everything that's happened? You still love me?"

His smile was half formed, and his bright green eyes were sad. "I'm afraid so. I can't stop thinking about you. I'm hoping you might love me back. I don't deserve your love or your forgiveness, but I'm hoping for them anyway."

She collapsed against him, holding him so close she could feel his breathing catch. "Yes, Clarke, I love you. Of course I do. I love you so much."

She didn't think his arms could tighten around her farther, but they did until she was almost unable to breathe from the pressure.

"Thank God for that. I'm still a risk. I've got to stay close to my program. I came right up to the edge and could have tumbled off easily. But I'm going to fight with everything I have. I have too much to lose." He kissed her forehead and then ran his hands over her head until they caught in her hair, and he tilted her face up to his again.

Terri ran her hands over his chest until she linked her fingers at the back of his neck. "I'll help." She wove her hands through his hair. "You were right. I don't take chances. I didn't take chances, but that ends now. I didn't want to risk my heart, and I almost lost you because of my fears. I've been closed and shut down, but I can change too. With your help. I love you." Apprehension drained out of her by inches. "I want to be someone different. I want to remember what it's like to be free with my feelings. I want to learn to be a chef and follow my passion. To hell with a steady job. I can find another if I need to. The worst I can do is fail, and I've got my MBA. I'd like to check out some meetings. I think I need them too. Oh, Clarke, I love you."

"That's great. I'll take you to a double winners meeting. They're for both alcoholics and Al-Anon. We can start there. The rest is up to you." He caressed her cheek until he was playing his thumb over her lower lip. She parted her lips for him, and with a sudden movement he kissed her, filling her mouth with his tongue as his hands held her hips against his. With a glad cry she pressed against him, passion in every line of his body as he claimed her with a possessive yet protective quality.

"I will. Thank you."

"Marry me, Terri. I want to be with you forever."

"Marry you?" She tried to hide her shock even while a pleased, satisfied feeling washed over her.

"I'm not letting you go, not ever." He shuddered. "I almost lost you. You have to marry me."

She drew back. "Oh, Clarke…"

He stopped her movements with an urgent squeeze. "Will you?" He studied her with a fierce question in his eyes that matched the intensity of his body.

"Yes. Of course. I love you."

He knelt and took her hands. "I will do everything I can to remind you every day that I love you. I'll make you happy." He rose, keeping his grip firm. She eased free and slid her arms around him again, pressing her head against his chest. He kissed the crown of her head, his breath hot.

"I'll do the same for you, as best I can."

"Then it's settled. We'll get married right after the gallery showing."

"That's a month from now. That doesn't give me enough time. It's impossible, Clarke!"

"A month," he said firmly. "I always assumed nothing was impossible. And since I have you by my side, I know that's true. I want the world to see you're mine, and I'm yours."

"Okay. I don't know how we're going to do it, but okay. Maybe Vegas?"

He shook his head. "No Vegas. A real wedding with a real ceremony. Whoever you want as witnesses. I'll figure something out. Kai, of course, and…others. Maybe Harris will stand up for me. Will your family come?" His tone was wistful.

"Of course. They wouldn't miss my marriage for anything. They'll be disappointed I'm not getting married in a field in a white Indian cotton dress and flowers in my hair, but they'll deal. They'll be there. They may take a while to warm up to you, but for my sake, they'll make the effort. That's how my family works."

His face twisted, and his eyes were sad. "I doubt my parents will come. My brother and sister might, and maybe my nieces. I'm not holding out much hope for my folks."

She tilted her face up to his. "If they don't, we'll create a new family. One we can always call our own."

"Oh, babe." He kissed her, drawing her tight around him and filling her with his presence.

The circle, which at one time had been an open loop, now closed. The future was spread out before them in glittering promise. Nothing could stop them from their dreams.

Epilogue

Ally Wilson joined Terri in front of the portrait that had been the object of her curiosity for so long. "Now that's love," Ally said, nudging her.

Terri glanced over at Clarke, resplendent in a dark brown designer suit with his hair brushed in gleaming waves and tied back in a short ponytail. Nobody would mistake this sleek, professional man for the disheveled addict of years past.

"Who would have believed ten years ago that this would ever happen?" She turned her attention back to the painting. "Clarke didn't want to show the picture, but I insisted." Her portrait held a conspicuous *Not for Sale* sign, and a rush of pride dashed through her.

Ally side-eyed her and then picked up Terri's hand to admire her ring. "You're lucky." She sighed, a mixture of envy and pleasure in the breath. For a moment Ally's expression was pensive, and then her face brightened. "Great ring."

Clarke's choice of a channel set diamond and ruby engagement ring sat on Terri's ring finger. The weight of the jewelry, both figurative and literal, had felt strange on her hand at first. Now she couldn't imagine being without his ring.

"I am." She peered behind Ally to the gallery beyond. "I was hoping to meet Dirk, the guy you're not dating."

Ally's scoff was a little too loud. "Not a chance. Dirk would rather chew his arm off than come to something like this. Besides, it's Sunday. Football is on."

Whatever private ideas she had about Ally's new friend were best kept to herself. The meetings she started to go to reminded her that she could only control her actions. Ally's love life was hers to manage.

The store was crowded beyond her expectations. Throngs of people were admiring Clarke's visions hung in simple frames on the walls throughout Ricki Stainer's gallery. The CD covers he'd designed for Kai were framed and arranged in a trio on the wall. Both already had *Sold* signs on them.

She wished Kai could have come to the reception, but he'd been called out of town with a Shatter Sound Records artist. Before he left, Kai had bought one of Clarke's latest paintings, a version of the Apposite Records logo with a suggestion of a panther in the background. Clarke had intended to give the painting to Kai, but Kai paid in cash before he could gift the piece to him.

"Tyris, there you are."

Ally gave a quick glance behind them and merged into the crowd as Terri's mother and father bore down on her. Rowenna August was in a flowing turquoise dress and matching jewelry. Her father, Martin, a quiet counterpart to her larger-than-life mother, stood behind the woman dripping in Southwest style rings and pendant.

"Hi, Mom. Dad."

Her mother swept her into a bear hug, clutching her daughter to her body before releasing her. "Wonderful event, Tyris. Wonderful."

Terri's father had a distracted appearance as he took in their surroundings.

"You resemble me in that picture." Rowenna August pointed with one silver-heavy finger toward the portrait. "We could be sisters."

"Twins," she agreed, her face solemn.

"I had dozens of men lining up to paint me, back in the day," her mother continued. "Just my luck I chose a man without an artistic bone in his body. Clarke will want me to pose for him, I am sure."

Terri's father looked a little pained but said nothing.

To her sorrow, Clarke's parents had not responded to the gallery invitation or the one for the wedding, but his brother and sister had. Terri had enrolled in the cooking school she dreamed of going to for all these years. Her training would take at least a year, and then she would try to get a job as a prep cook and work her way up. Consulting would fill the void where needed. Without the encouragement of Kai and Clarke, she wasn't sure she would have had the strength to take that leap.

She spotted Harris, who was more interested in talking to the nubile young thing standing by the canvas than the painting itself. They had plans for Clarke to record a song on Harris and Steve's album. She hoped that would erase any lingering ugliness from the old wounds.

"I am sure he will, Mom."

Her father spoke for the first time. He reached into the battered satchel he carried, removed a bundle, and handed the papers to her. "We bought you a present."

She regarded the envelope, which bore the imprint of the school she was about to attend. Her brow furrowing, she opened the package to find an ornate wedding card. Inside was a receipt for the full tuition of her culinary program.

Words failed her for several moments. "I...this wasn't necessary," she said after a long pause.

"Nonsense." Her mother waved any objection away, her jewelry jangling with the movement. "Tyris, you will be a brilliant chef. We didn't want you to struggle and work while you were going to school. You have to concentrate. After you graduate, you can go on one of those cooking shows. You're my daughter; you're bound to win."

Terri hugged her parents, tears gathering. The door to the gallery opened, and an older couple stepped through. Something about them caught her attention, and she moved back from her father to watch them. They glanced around, appearing nervous and out of place. Then their gazes fell on Clarke, and the man nudged the woman.

Her breath stopped. The resemblance to her fiancé should have been apparent right away. She recognized the couple from pictures of Clarke's early life. He hadn't spotted the newcomers yet; his attention was still focused on the woman. Rowenna caught her eye, and Terri gestured with her chin to the other couple.

She crossed the room to Clarke and tugged on his sleeve. Her parents were close behind. He murmured something to the woman, kissed her hand, and turned to Terri with a puzzled air. Instead of words, she spun him in the direction of the front door and pushed gently.

Clarke stopped when he saw the people, his body

going still. His fingers sought hers and closed tight as if they were a lifeline. Squeezing his hand, Terri pushed at him again.

He swallowed. "Come with me."

She nodded and glanced at her parents. Rowenna opened her mouth to say something, but Martin pressed her arm, and she remained quiet.

A server was handing them champagne as Clarke made his way toward the man and woman who could only be his parents through the thick crowd. They stood together, holding the glasses in front of them. A horrified look crossed his mother's face when she noted what she had in her hand. She summoned a waitress, and they got rid of the glasses.

The ebb and swell of the conversation flowed around them. A faint scent of paint overlaid the odors of finger foods, shrimp, and humans. His parents' eyes never wavered from Clarke. Clarke's mother fidgeted, twining a lock of short gray hair around her fingers.

"Mom, Dad, hi. Thanks for coming."

His father's throat worked, and his face crumpled just a bit, a motion almost too small to be detected. Then he straightened and focused on Clarke.

"You're welcome." A hint of Clarke's familiar burr was in the man's tone.

"Guys, I want you to meet Terri. My fiancée." He sounded proud, happy, and her emotions swelled.

Regret was in the older man's eyes, so much like Clarke's but faded with the advancement of time. She could forgive them for not responding, because they were at the gallery. Forgiving them for hurting the man she loved was going to take longer. She murmured something she hoped was polite and shook their hands.

His father, who Terri understood was named Warren, studied her for many moments. "Congratulations. Are we too late to RSVP for the wedding?"

Clarke met and held her gaze, asking her the question without words. She mentally reworked the seating arrangements and the food and then gave him a quick nod. He let out a sigh of relief.

"Of course you aren't too late," Clarke said. "We're glad you can come. Thank you." He slipped his arm around Terri and hugged her.

"I'm Rowenna. Tyris's mother." Her mother made no move to touch the other man. Her expression said she was withholding judgment on these new in-laws. "We'll be family soon. We are so happy for this adorable couple. Our daughter is an amazing woman. Your son is a fortunate man." Her jewelry jangled as Rowenna talked, and her mother's face was set in cautious lines.

Terri smiled, recognizing the glare as the one Kai had called her "Terrible Terri." She had picked up some traits from her parents. His parents nodded like bobble heads, their faces equally as frozen.

"I'm very lucky." Clarke's voice vibrated with a myriad of emotions. "I love this woman. Exchanging vows will be the best thing I ever did." He gazed at the people clustered around them. "Come on. Let me show you my work."

Clarke and Terri began walking around the room, their families close behind. They were together. More than that, they were showing both sides their commitment to their new beginning and to each other. Their coming together was going to be a big, messy transition. Terri was sure words would be exchanged and tears would be shed. That was how life went sometimes.

The second act of their lives had begun.

A word about the author…

Claire can't remember a time when writing wasn't part of her life. Growing up, she used to write stories with her friends. As a teenager she started out reading fantasy and science fiction, but her diet quickly changed to romance and happily-ever-after.

A native of Massachusetts and cold weather, she left all that behind to move to the sun and fun of California, but has always lived no more than twenty miles from the ocean.

In college she studied acting with a minor in creative writing. In hindsight she should have flipped course studies. Before she was published, she sold books on eBay and discovered some of her favorite authors by sampling the goods.

While she's not a movie mogul or actor, she does work in the film industry with her office firmly situated in the 90210 district of Hollywood.

Prone to break out into song, she is quick on her feet and just as quick with snappy dialogue. In addition to writing she does animal rescue, reads, and goes to movies. She loves to hear from fans, so feel free to drop her a line.

~*~

Find Claire online at:
http://www.clairedavon.com

Thank you for purchasing
this publication of The Wild Rose Press, Inc.

For questions or more information
contact us at
info@thewildrosepress.com.

The Wild Rose Press, Inc.
www.thewildrosepress.com